Pokémon™

Find 'Em All!

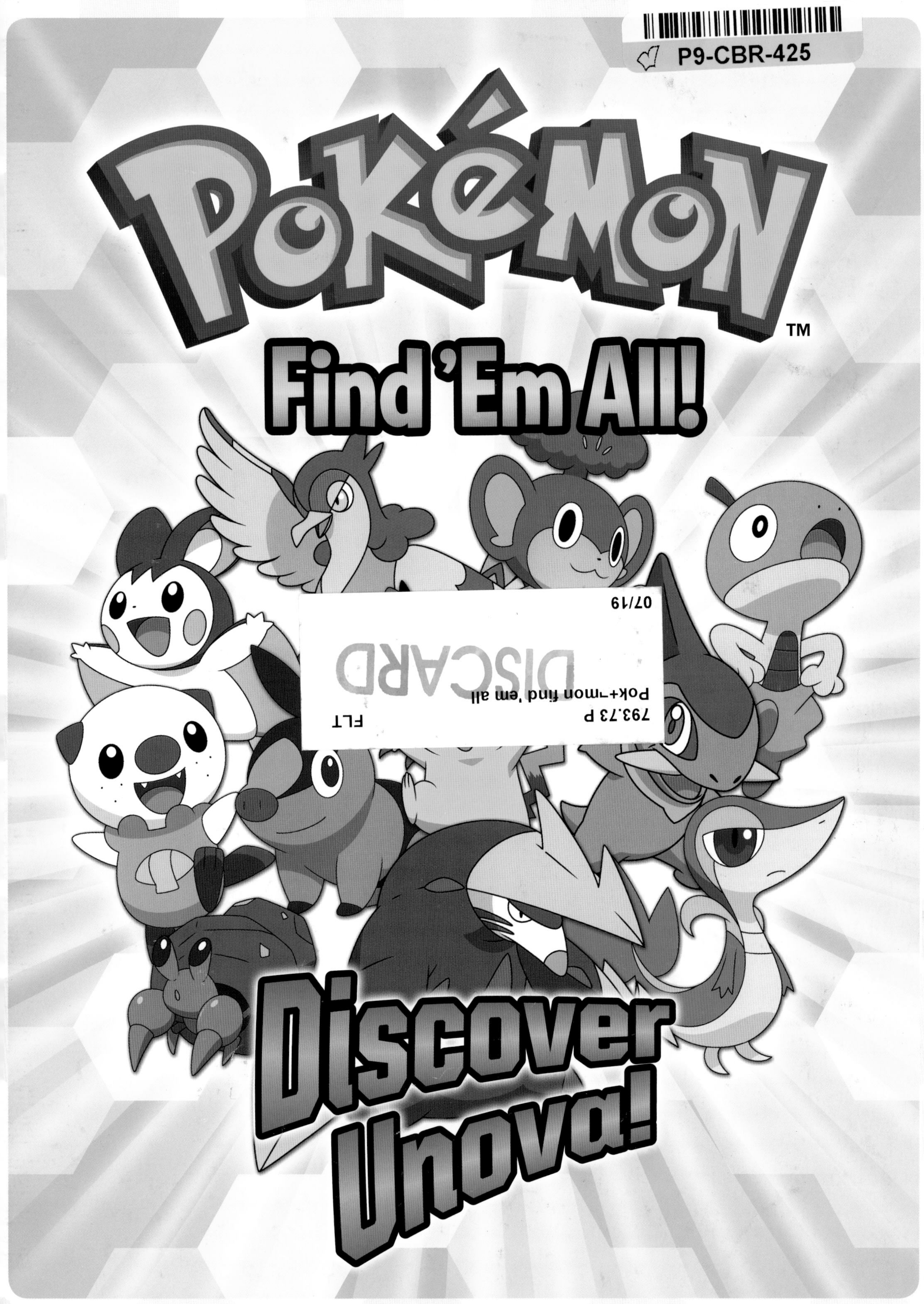

Discover Unova!

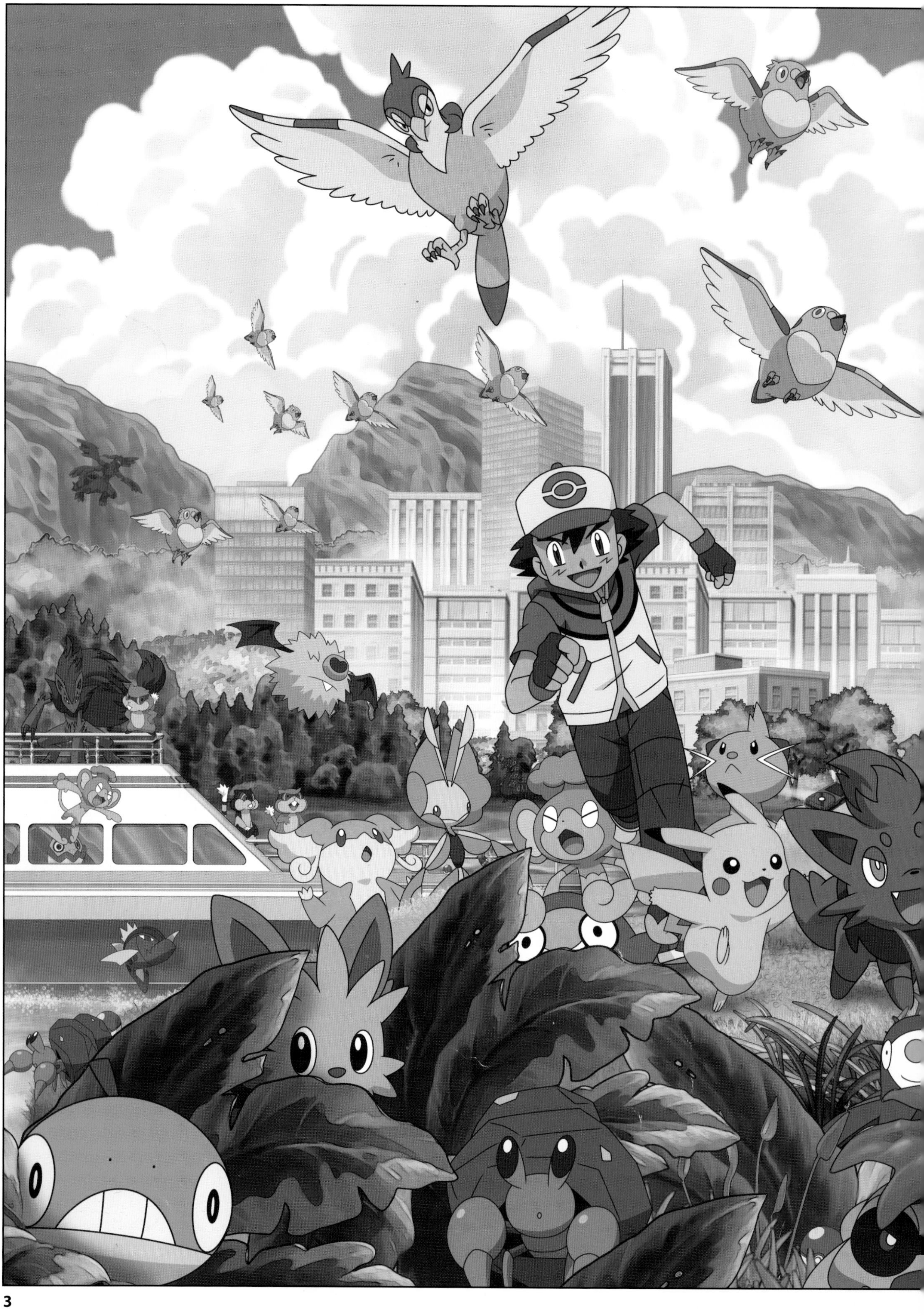

ARRIVING IN UNOVA

Ash and Pikachu have just arrived in the Unova region! They're very excited to discover Pokémon they've never seen before living here. And Watchog, Patrat, and Pidove are watching as these new visitors arrive. So, let's start exploring Unova!

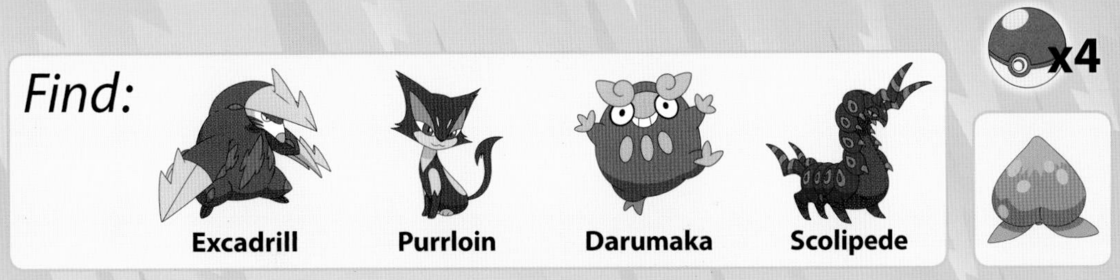
Find:
Excadrill
Purrloin
Darumaka
Scolipede
x4

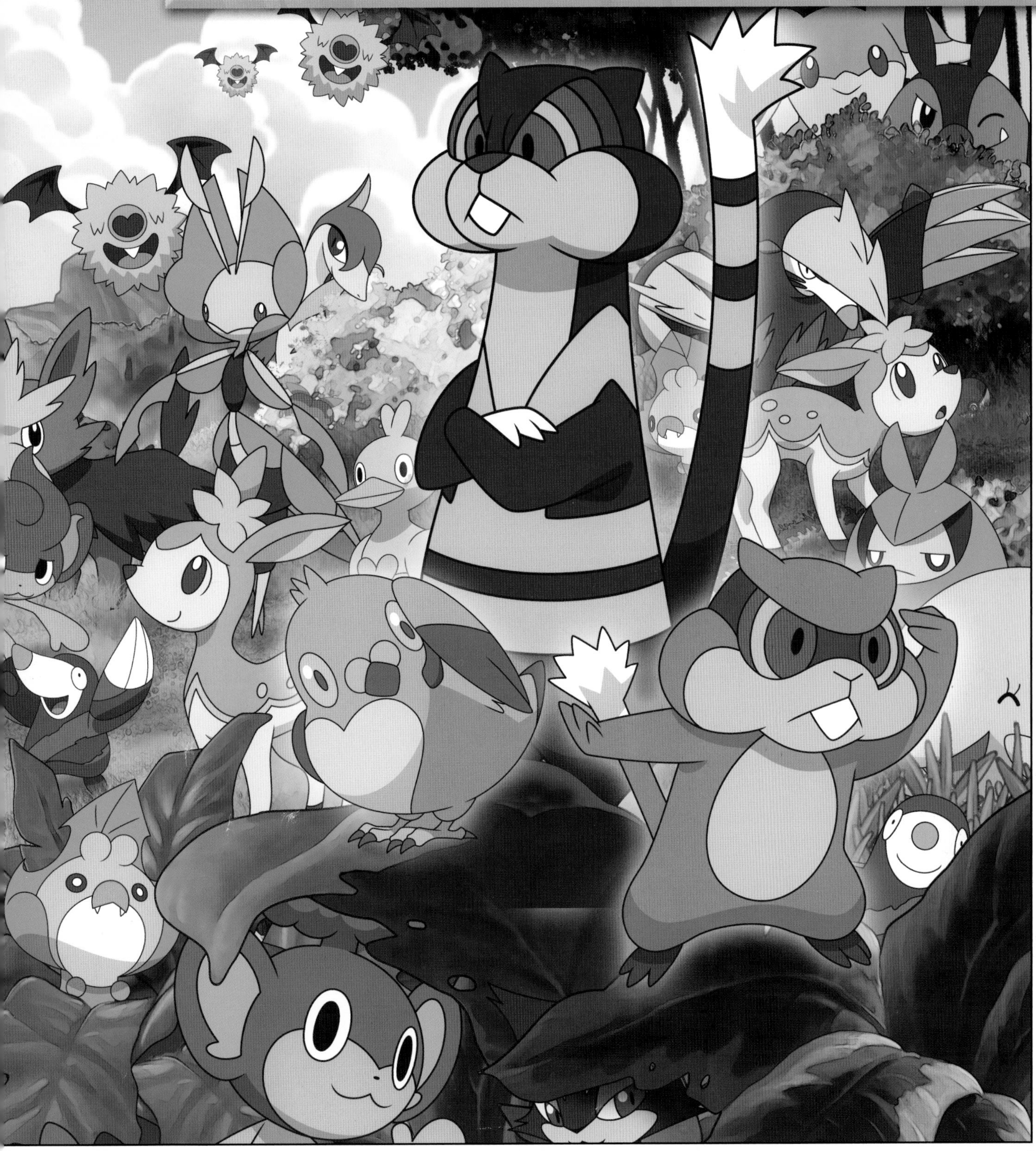

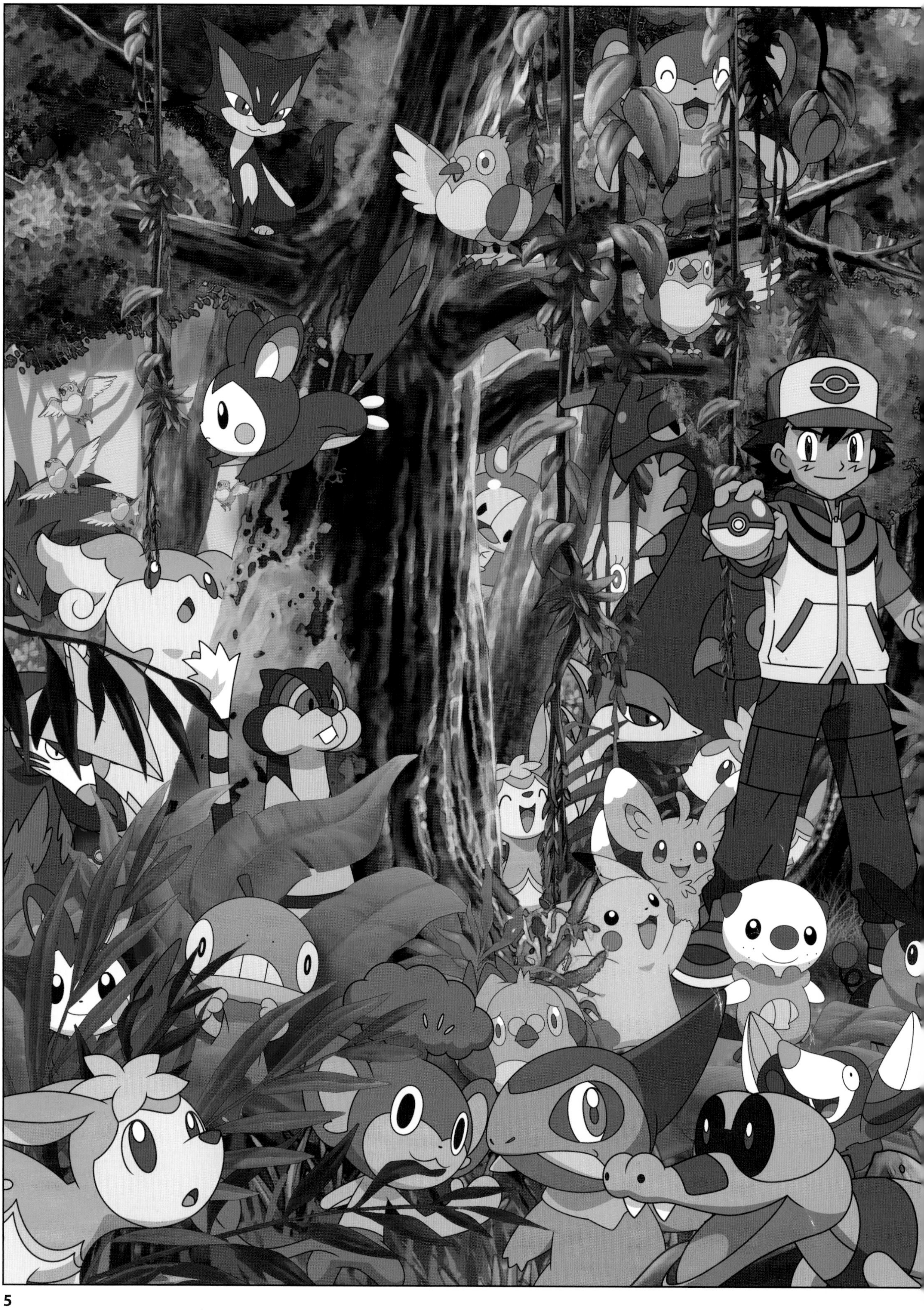

IN THE HEART OF THE FOREST

To reach to the nearest town, Ash decides to walk through the forest. It's the best way to discover what Pokémon live in this area, such as Grass- or Bug-types. There are three wonderful examples here: Sewaddle, Swadloon, and Leavanny. This journey certainly looks educational!

Find:

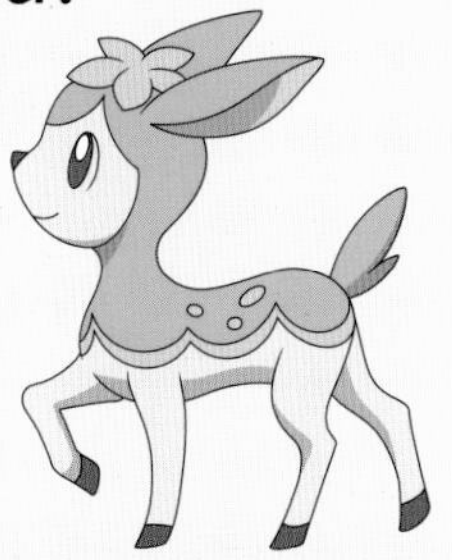

Deerling x4

x8

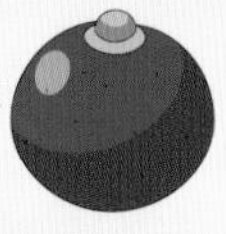

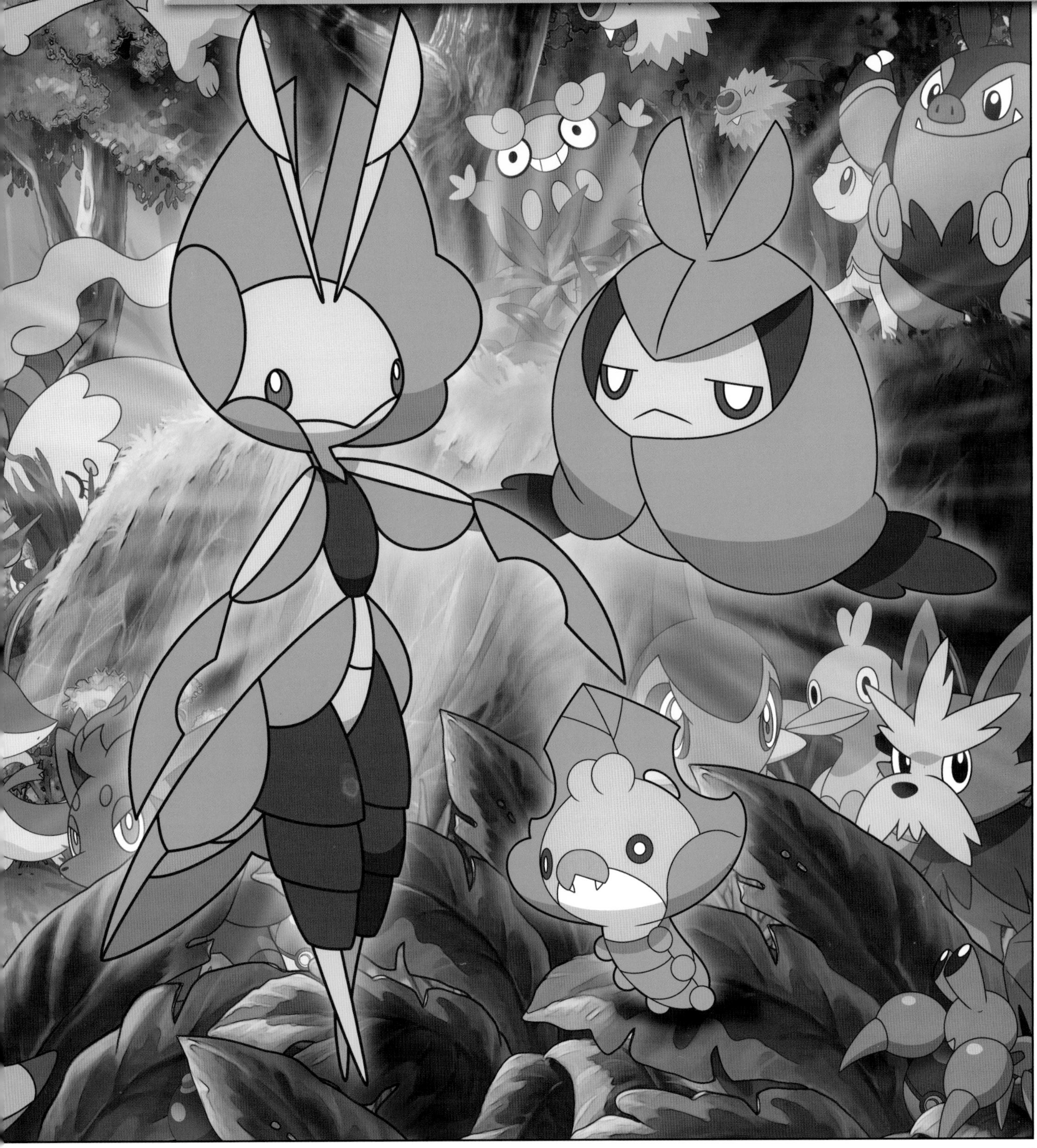

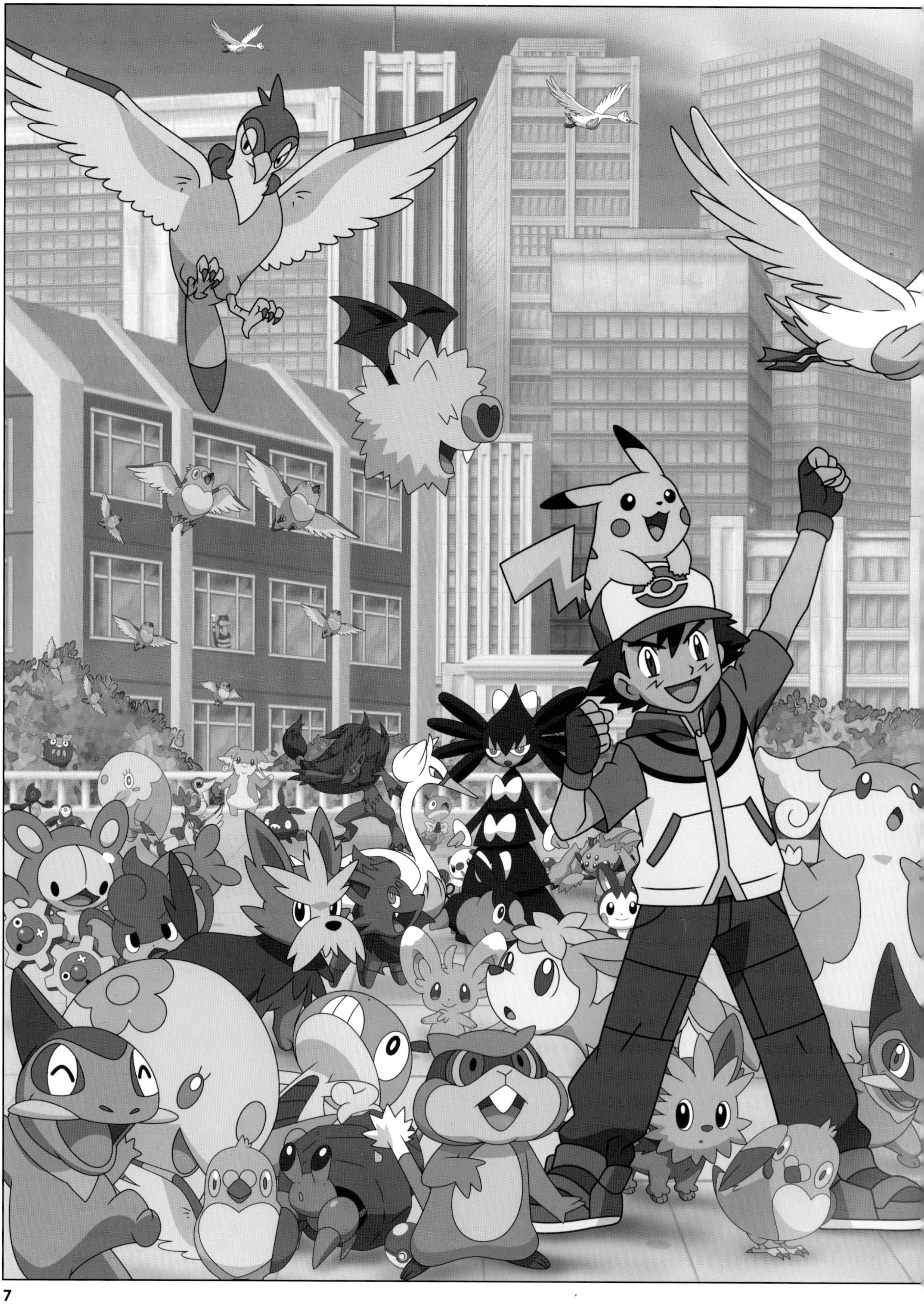

EXPLORING THE TOWN

Ash goes from surprise to surprise. He is particularly amazed by three Pokémon: Servine, Pignite, and Dewott. He wants to know everything about them and hopefully battle them in a tournament. The best way to make this happen is to find the nearest Pokémon Center for more information…

Find:

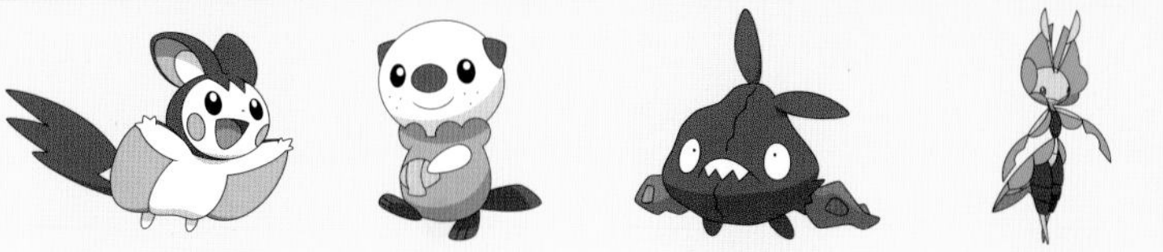

Emolga | Oshawott | Trubbish | Leavanny

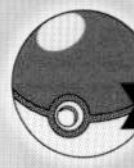

x3

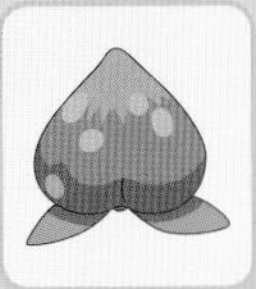

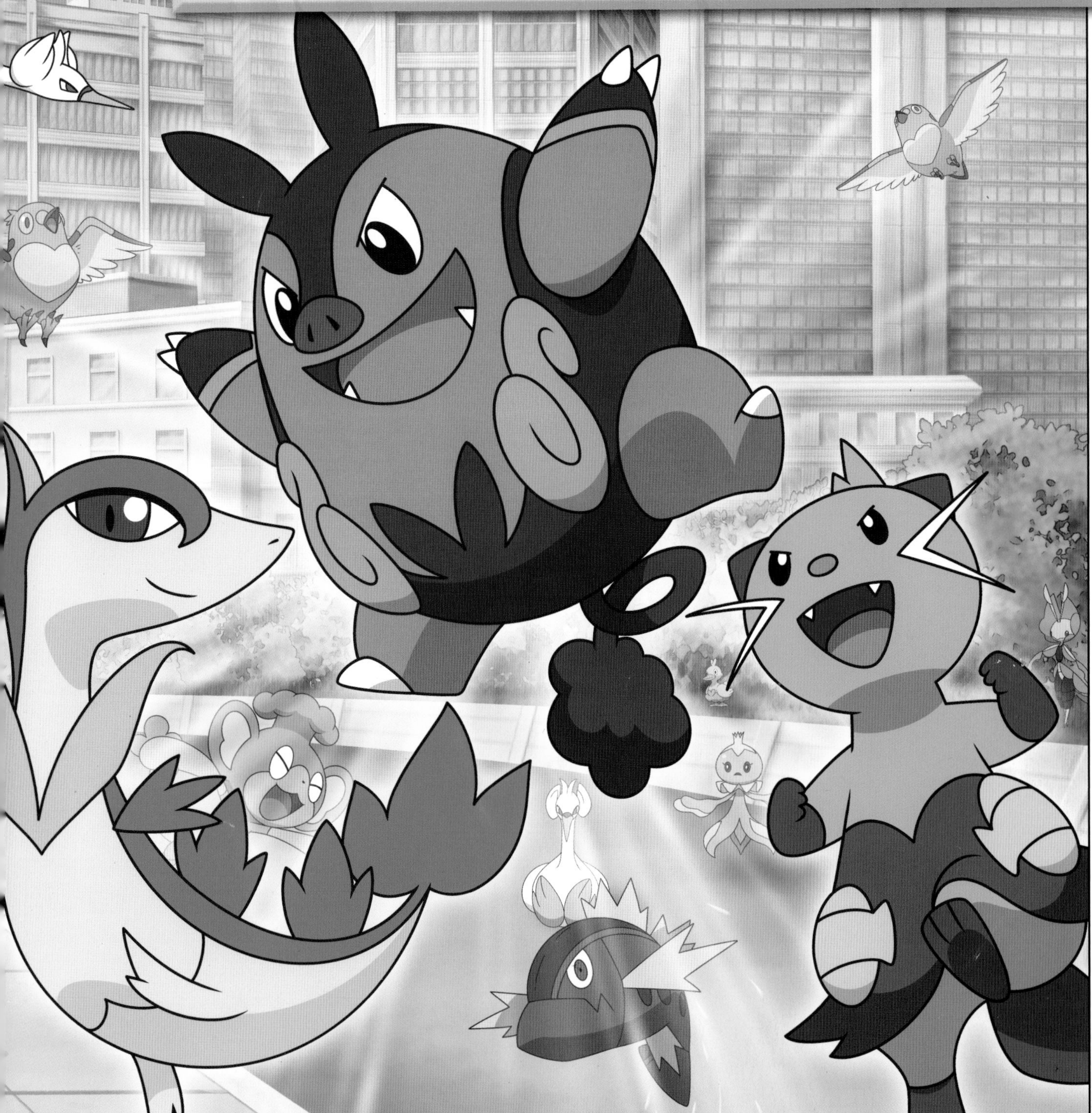

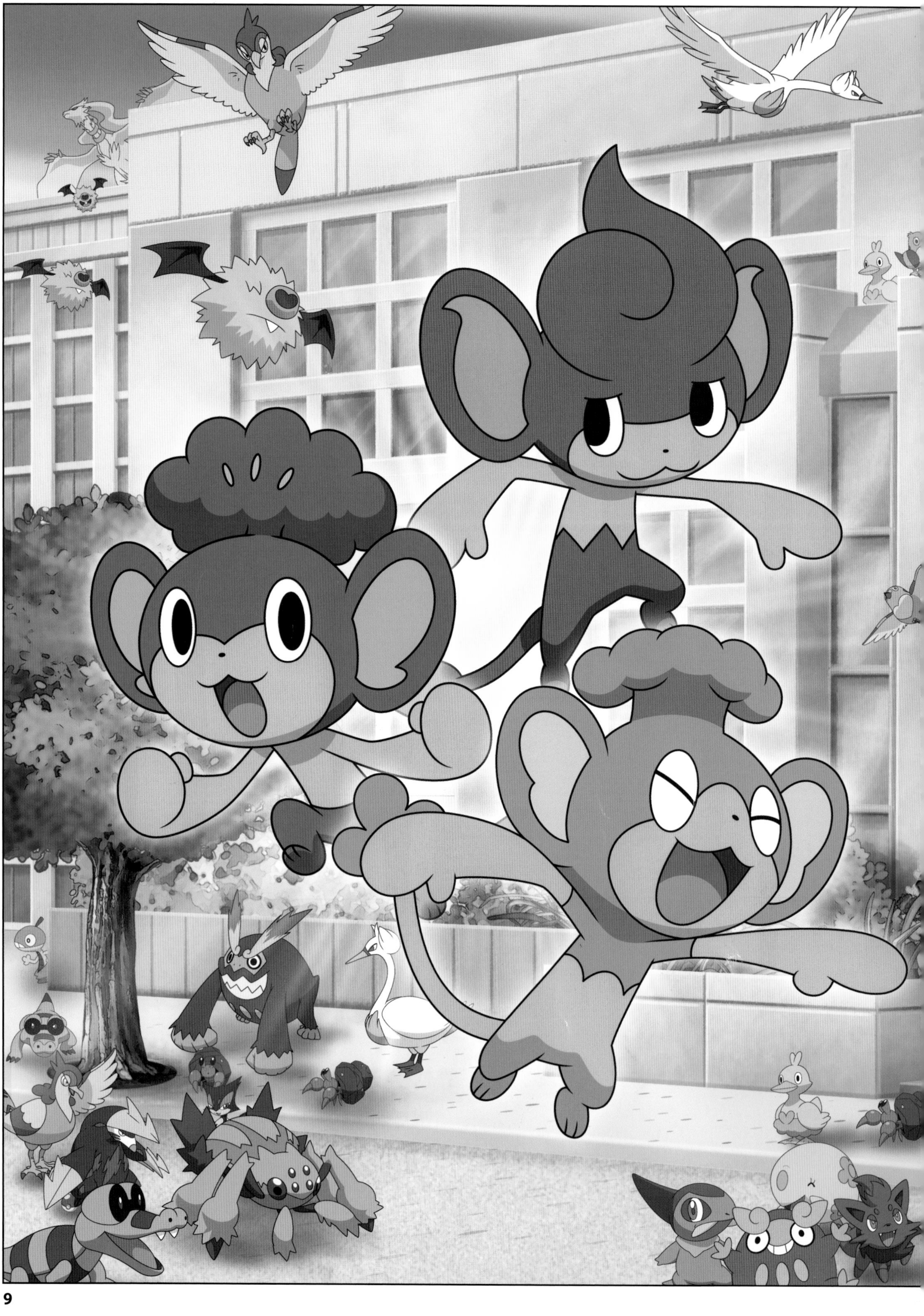

AT THE POKÉMON CENTER

We made it! Someone at the Pokémon Center is bound to know about the various tournaments around the Unova region. Ash is determined to learn more, but in the meantime, these three friendly Pokémon—Pansage, Pansear, and Panpour—have really grabbed his attention!

Find:

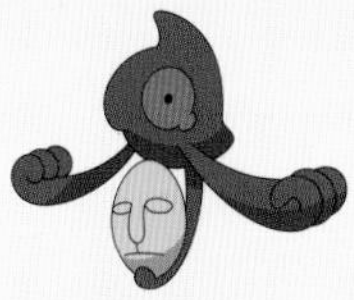
Yamask

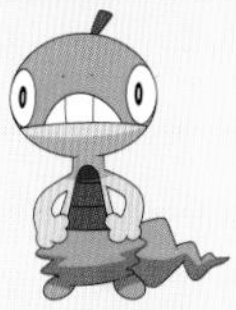
Scraggy

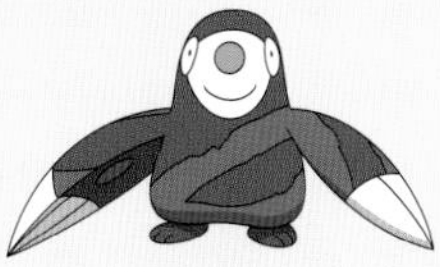
Drilbur

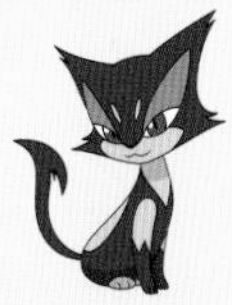
Purrloin

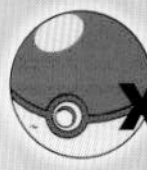
x6

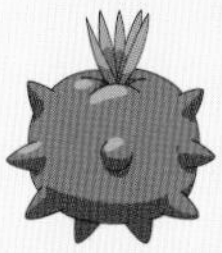

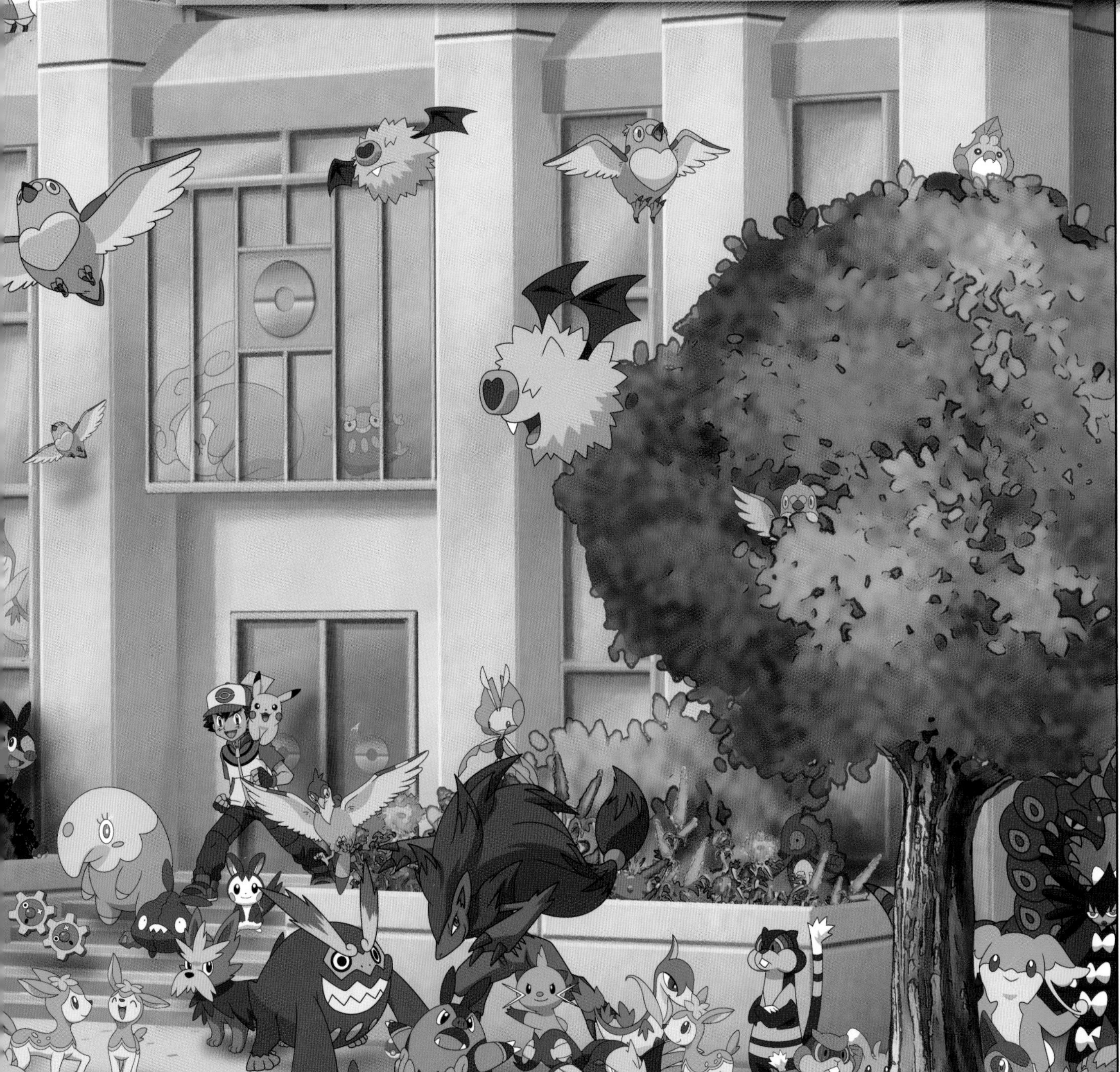

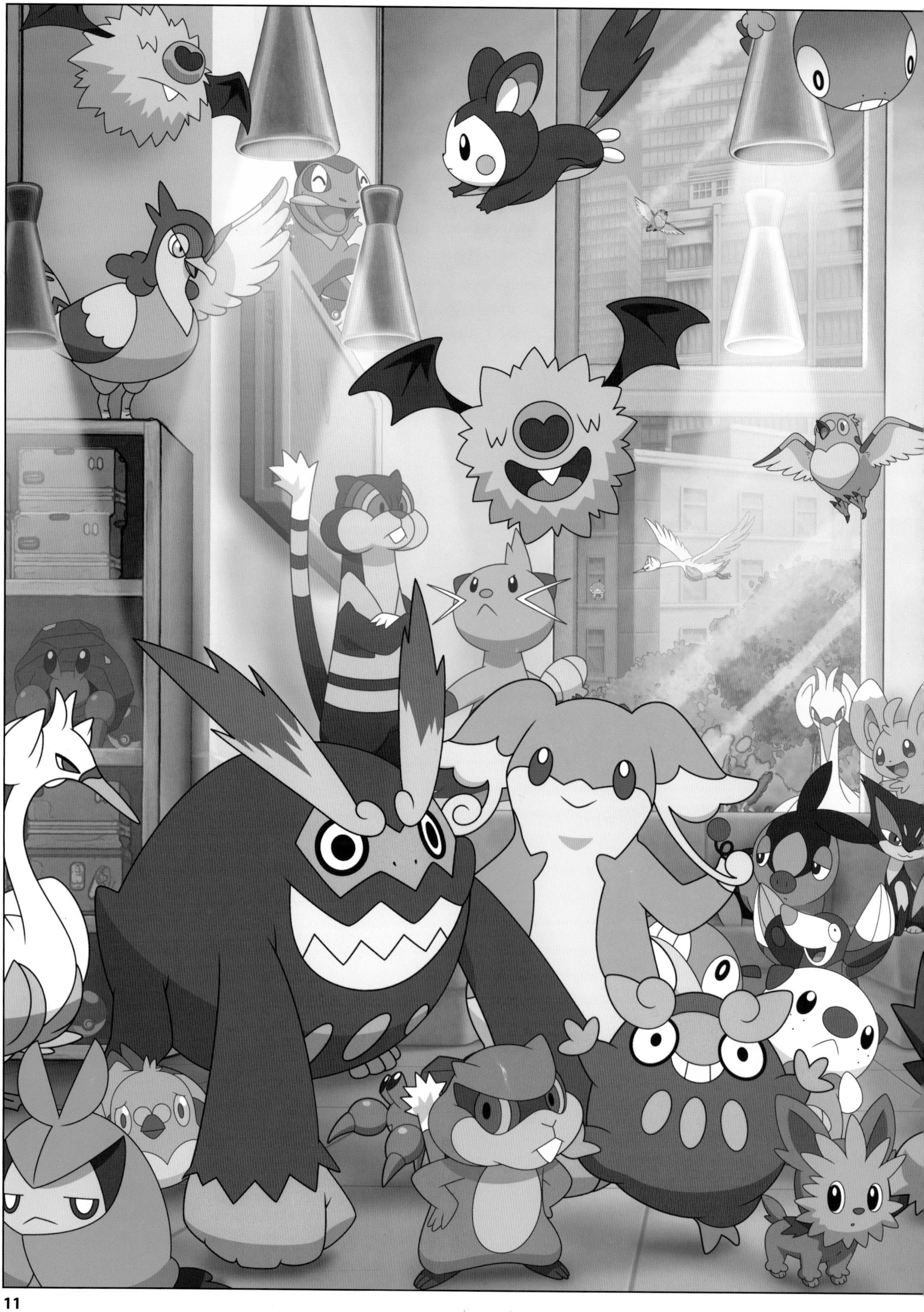

POKÉMON CENTER CHAOS

This Pokémon Center is so crazy! What's going on here? Ash learns about a large tournament in town taking place tomorrow, and, of course, everyone wants to be in top form. That must be why it's so busy here! Ash and Pikachu are lucky: they arrived at the best time to check out the strengths of their future opponents!

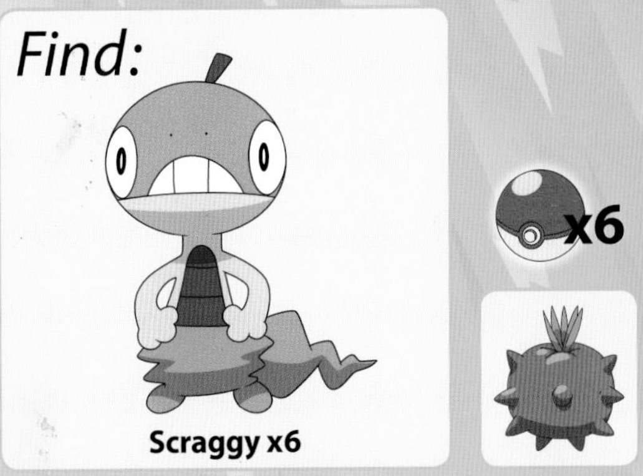
Find:
Scraggy x6
x6

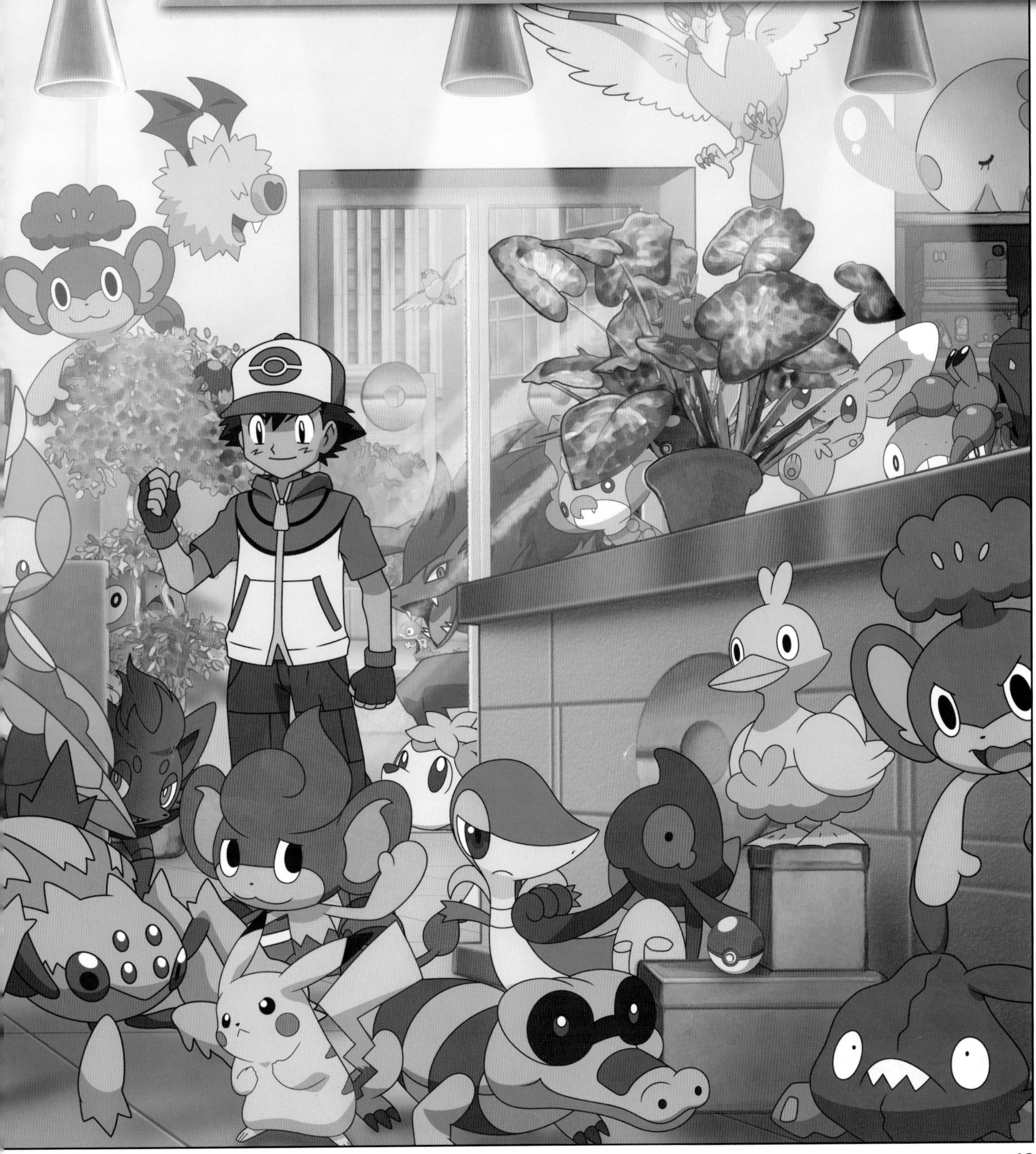

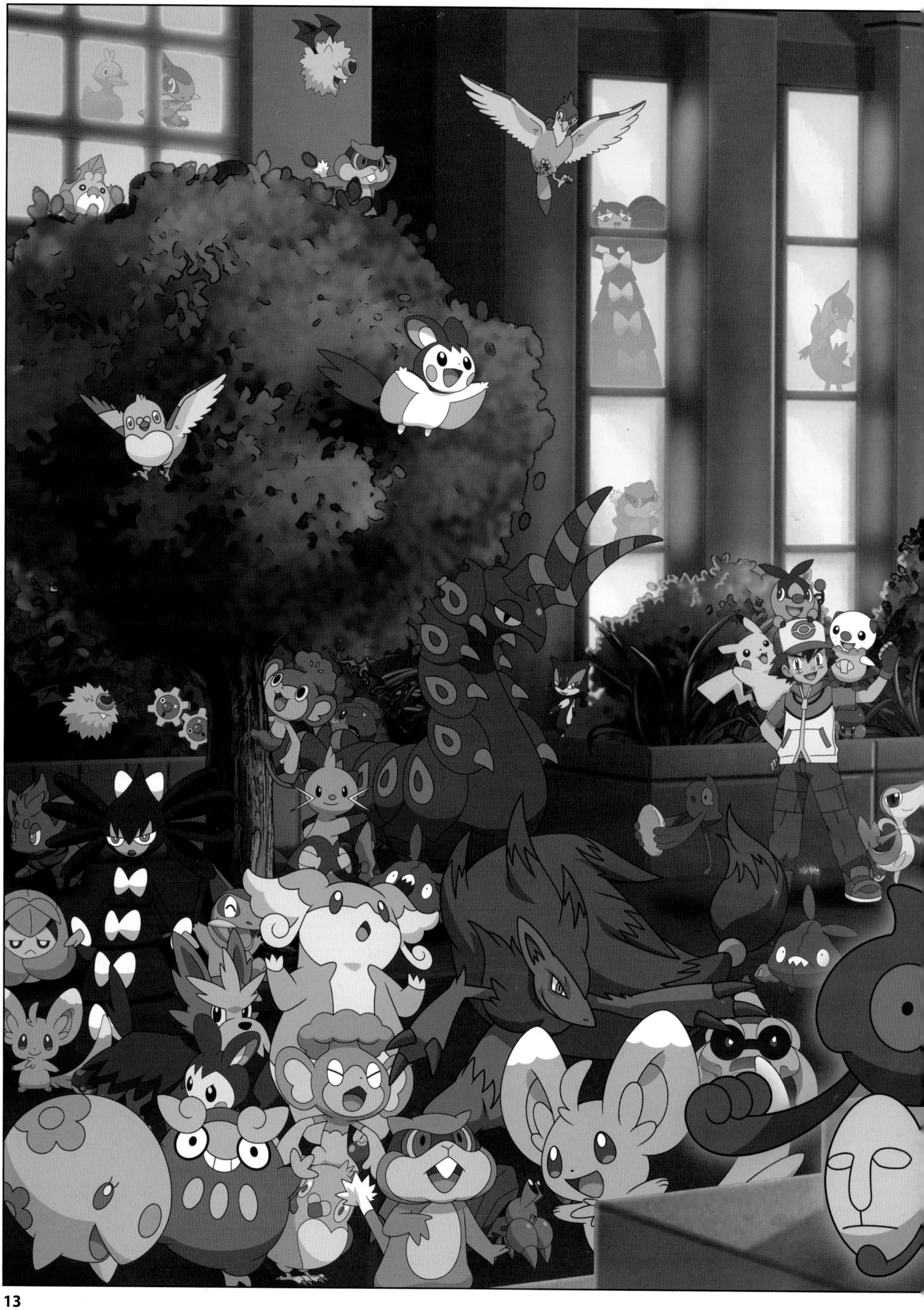

AFTER DARK

Ash spent so much time in the Pokémon Center to get ready for tomorrow's tournament that it's already dark by the time he leaves. But that's good! This will give him the chance to find more Ghost- or Dark-type Pokémon, such as Yamask, Purrloin, Zorua, Scraggy, or Sandile.

Find:

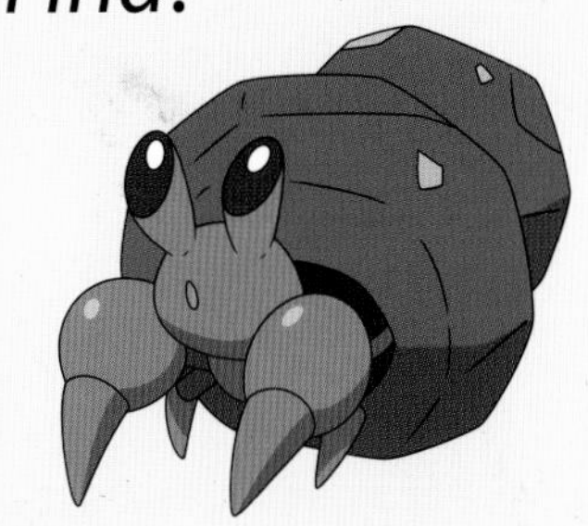

Dwebble x5

x5

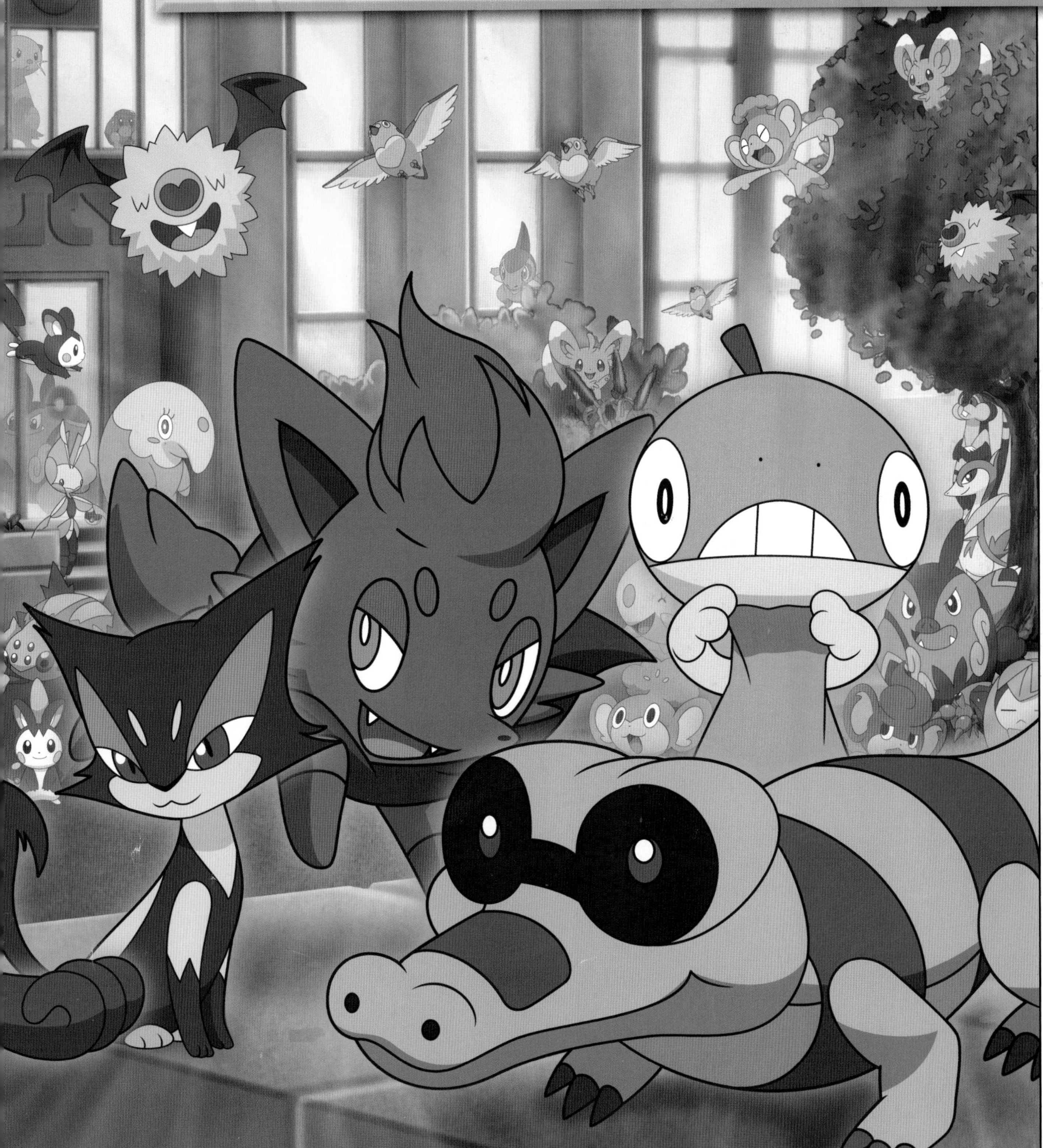

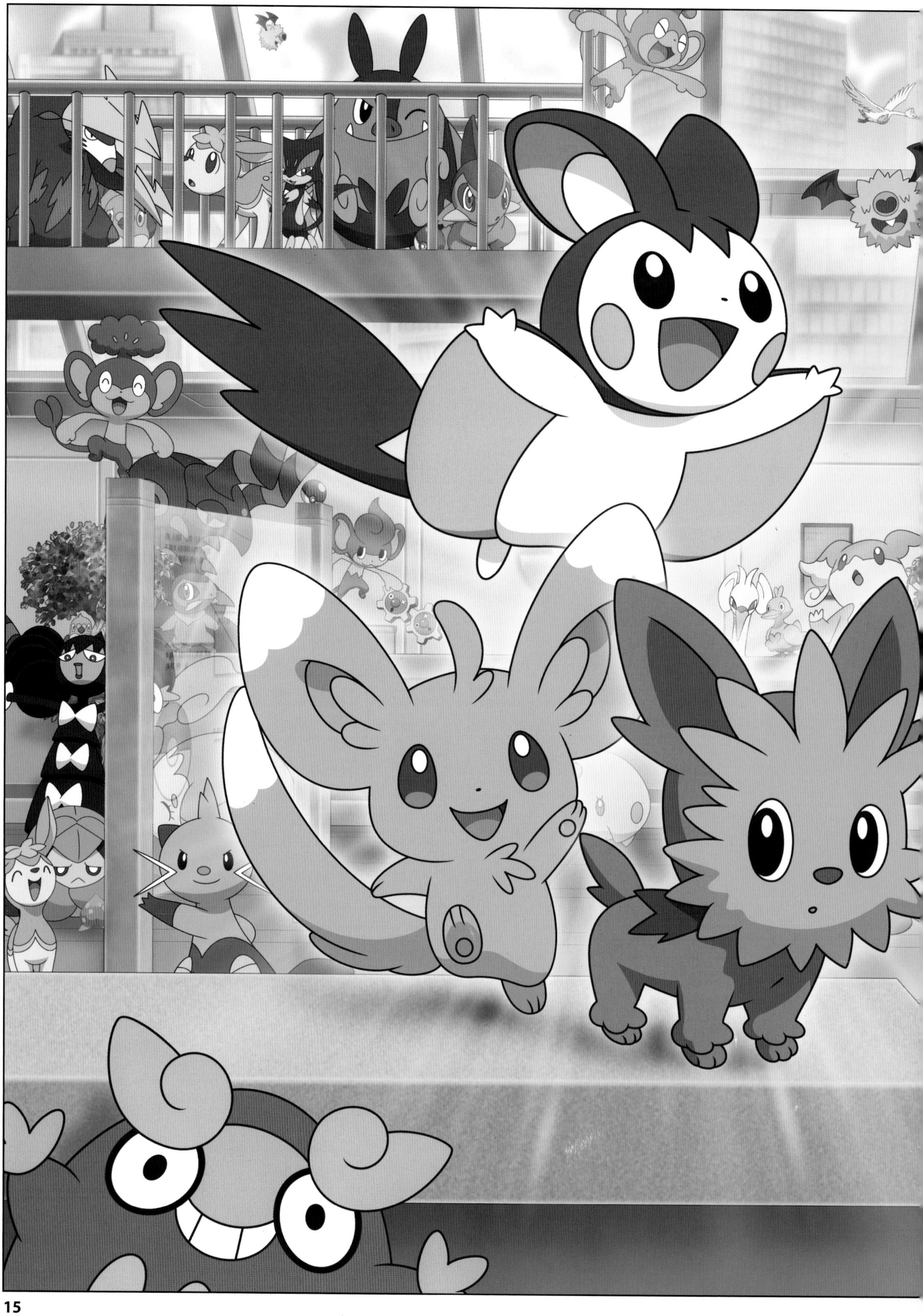

TIME FOR THE BATTLE CLUB

It's finally time! Ash arrived early to register for the tournament, but many Pokémon are already here! Some of his opponents look very serious, but it takes more than just looks to intimidate Ash and Pikachu. Three Pokémon in particular—Emolga, Minccino, and Lillipup—look adorable, but Ash knows that you can't judge an opponent's strength by its appearance!

Find:

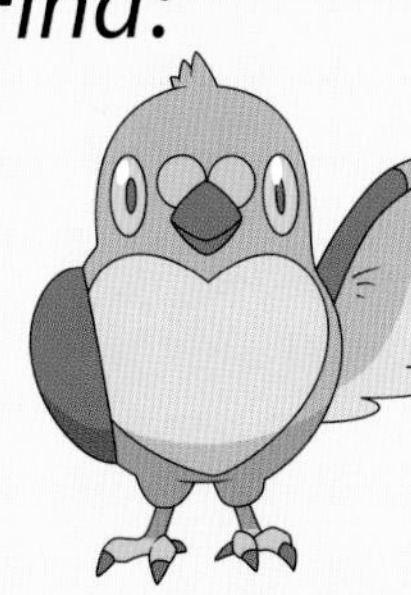

Pidove x5

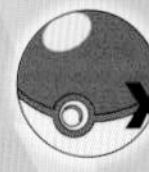

x6

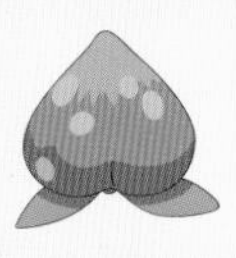

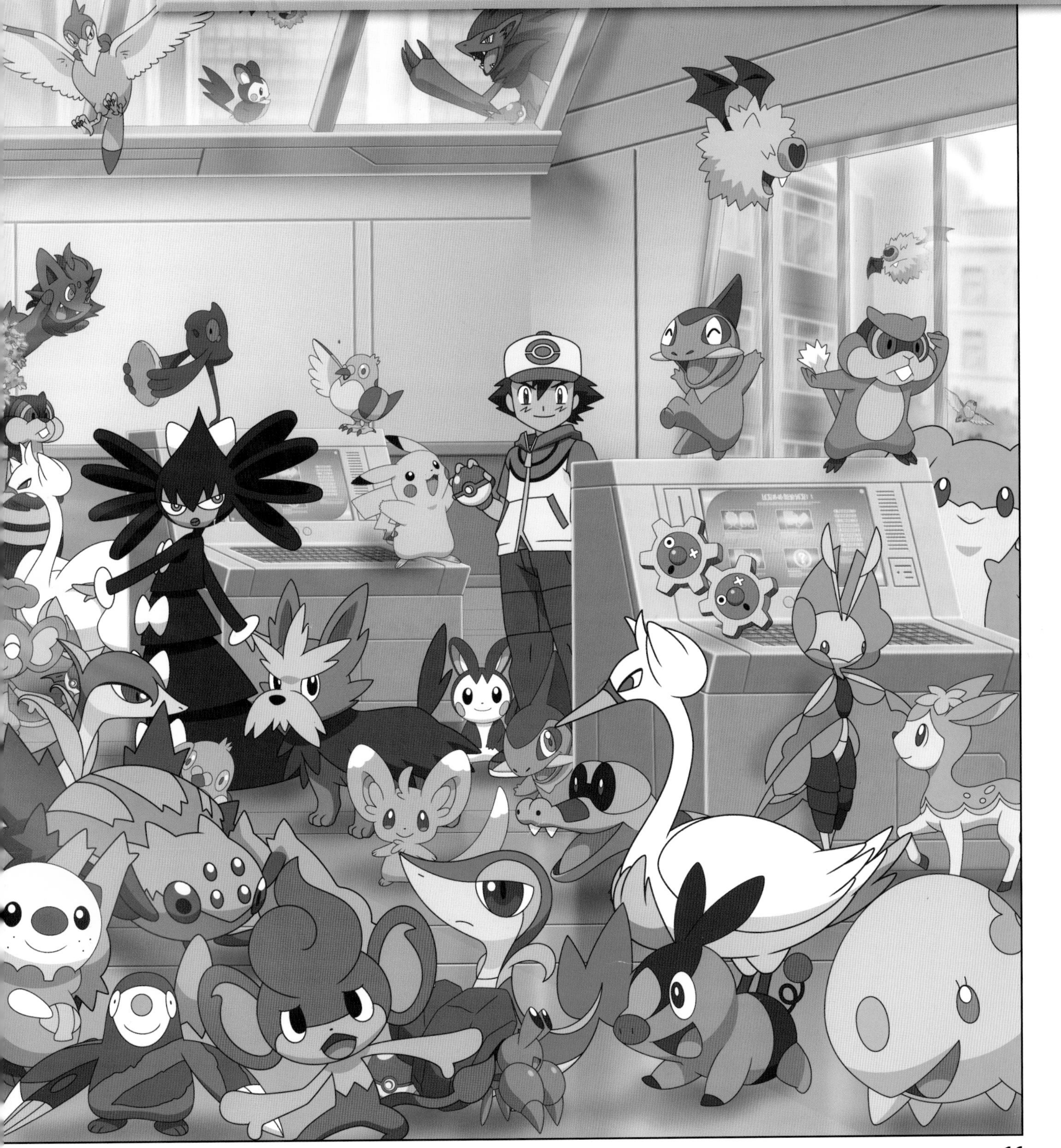

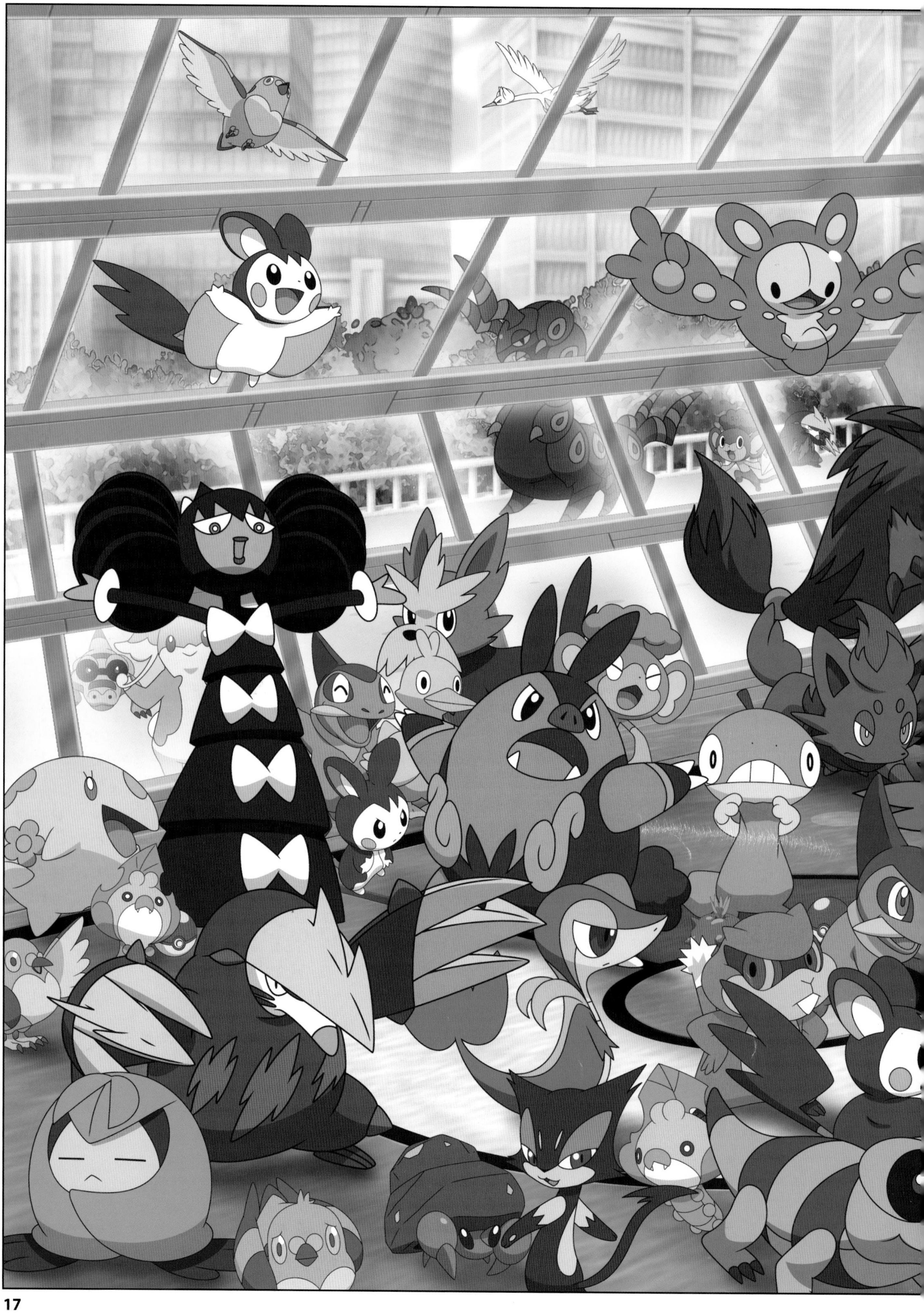

THE TRAINING ROOM

Before diving into battle, Ash wants to spend some time in the training room. It's a good way to learn about other Pokémon's strengths and strategies, and it looks like Pikachu will have to face some strong competition! Ash's battles in Unova have only just begun!

Find:

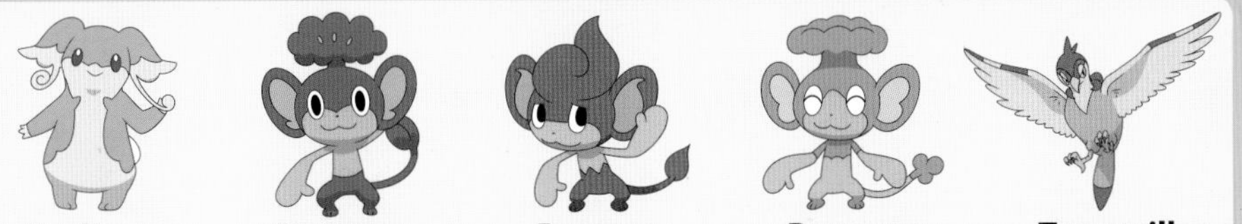

Audino Pansage Pansear Panpour Tranquill

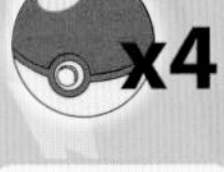
x4

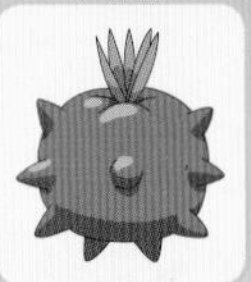

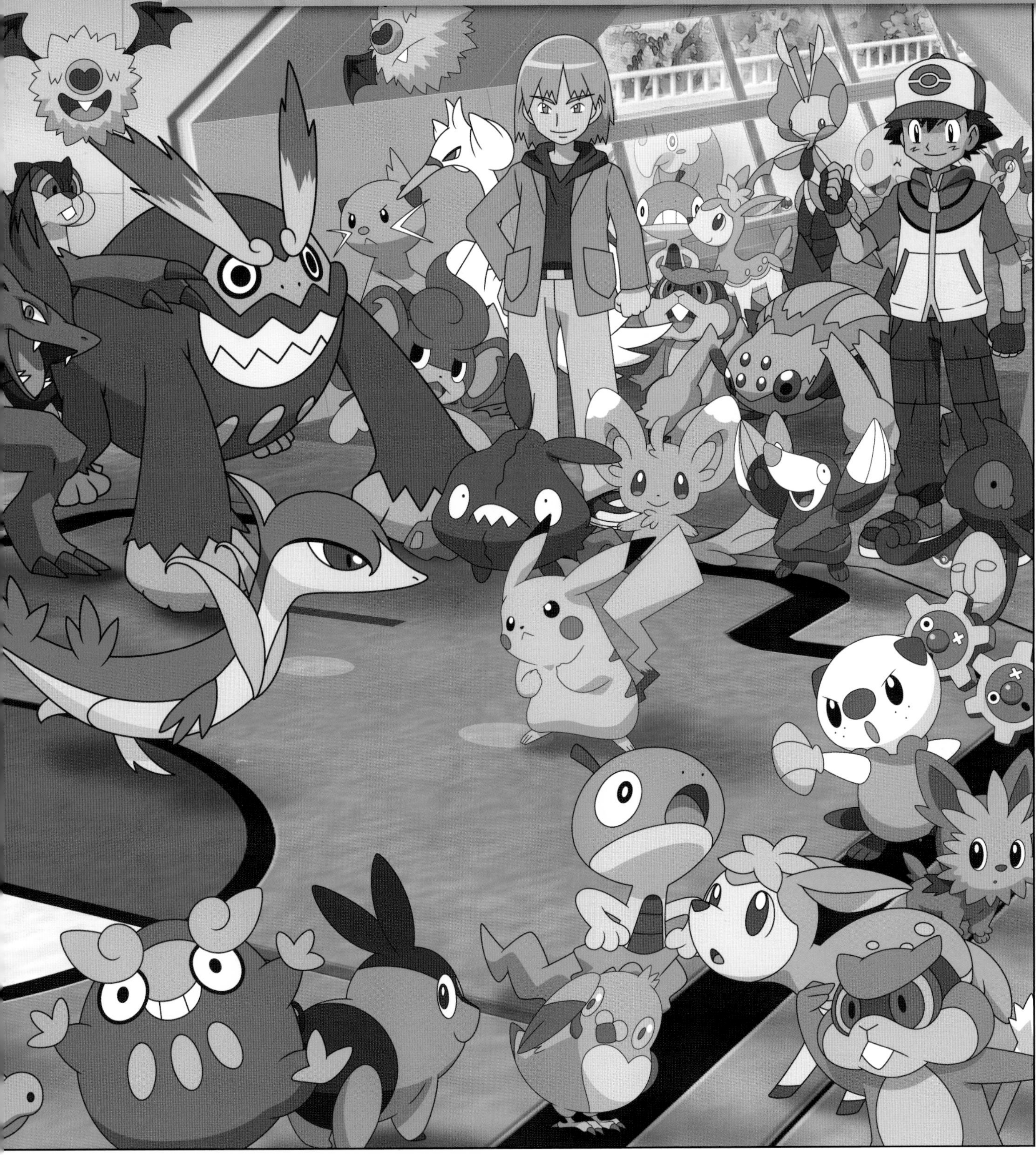

NEW CHALLENGES

Have you completed every search and found all the Poké Balls?

Then you're ready for these two new challenges that only the best Pokémon Trainers can take on!

⊙ THE LEGENDARY CHALLENGE

Two Legendary Pokémon are hiding somewhere in these pages of adventure. Can you find them?

Reshiram

Zekrom

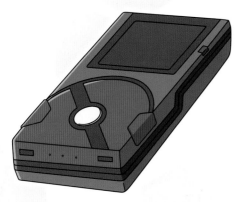

⊙ THE SUPREME CHALLENGE

During his adventure, Ash dropped his Pokédex, which allows him to collect data and learn all about Pokémon. Help him figure out where he lost it!

POKéMON™

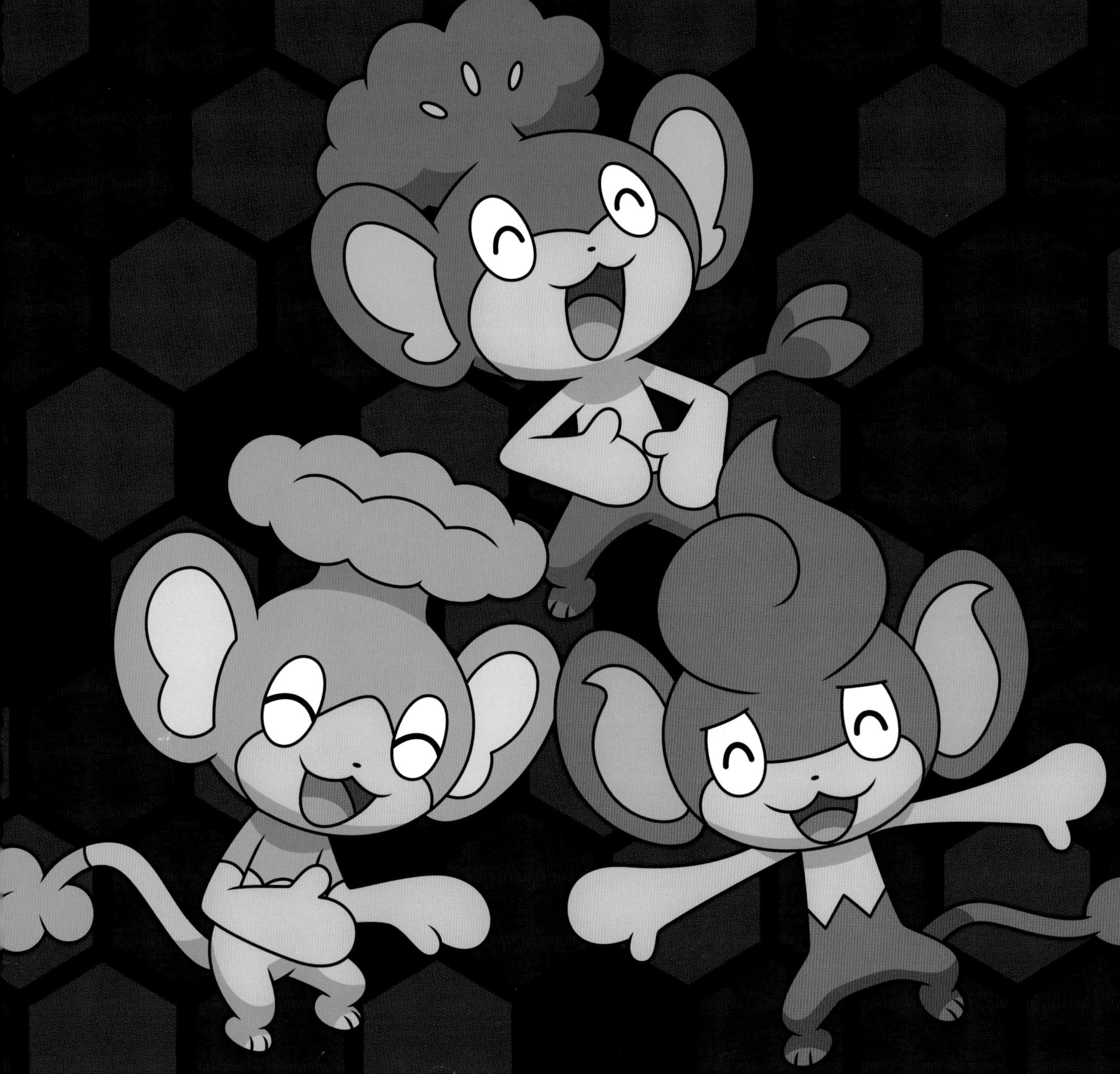

RESHIRAM

When the flames in Reshiram's tail flare, the thermal energy generated changes the atmosphere and alters weather patterns all around the world.

TYPE: Dragon-Fire
ABILITY: Turboblaze
HEIGHT: 10' 06" / 3,2m
WEIGHT: 725.5lbs. / 330,0kg

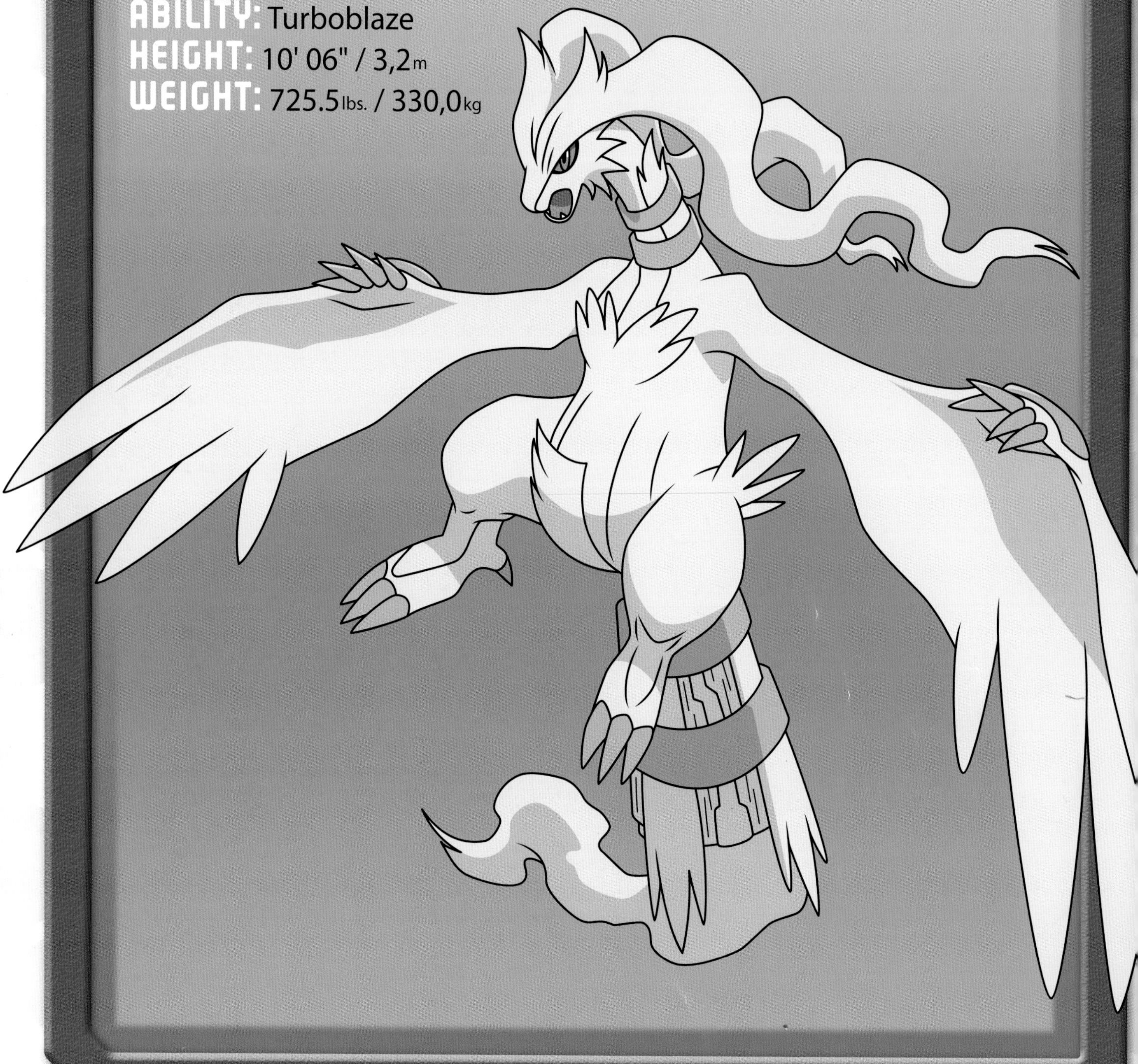

ZEKROM

Concealing itself in lightning clouds, it flies throughout the Unova region. In its tail, it has a giant generator that creates electricity.

TYPE: Dragon-Electric
ABILITY: Teravolt
HEIGHT: 9' 06" / 2,9m
WEIGHT: 760.6lbs. / 345,0kg

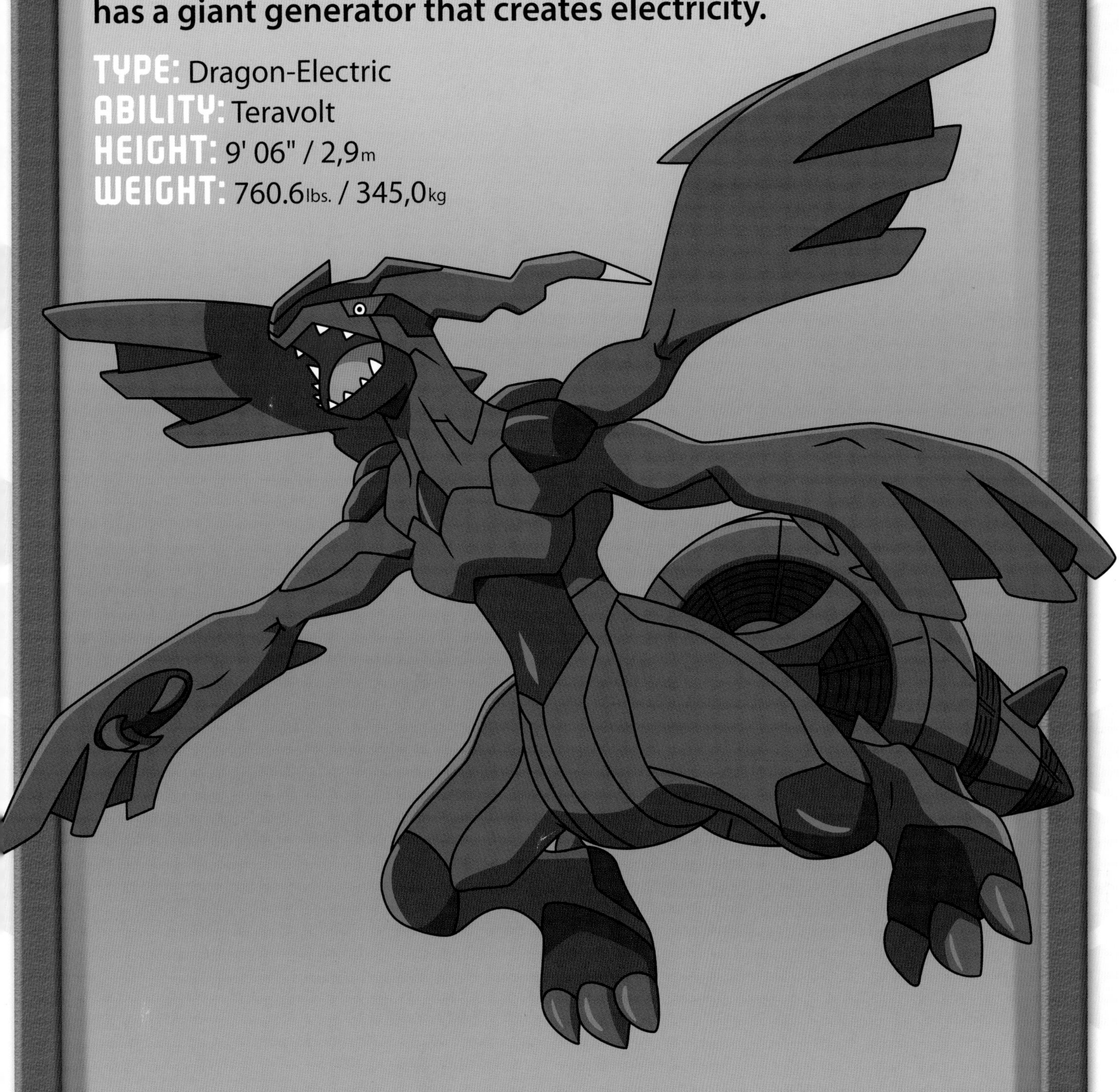

SOLUTIONS

ARRIVING IN UNOVA 3–4

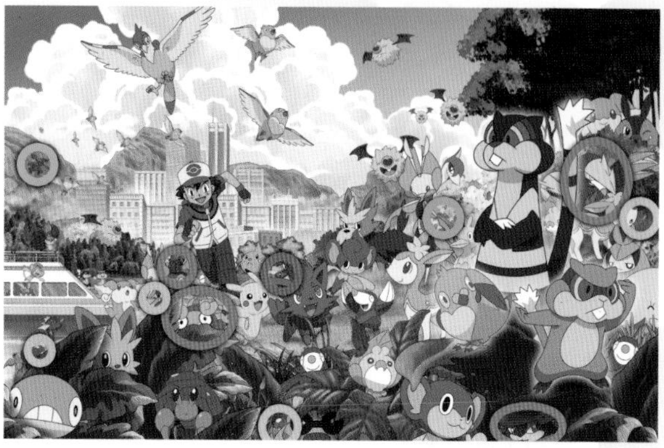

IN THE HEART OF THE FOREST 5–6

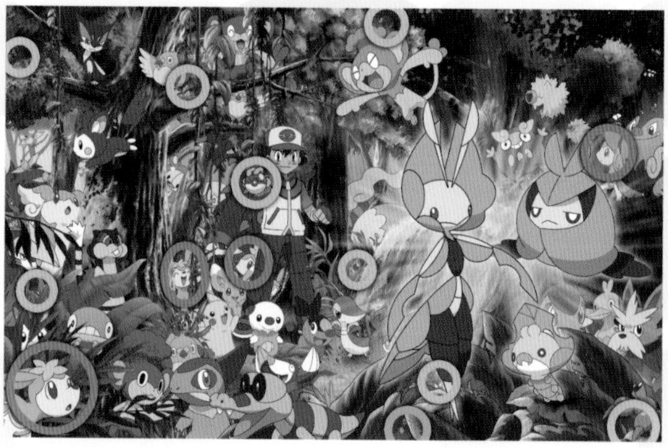

EXPLORING THE TOWN 7–8

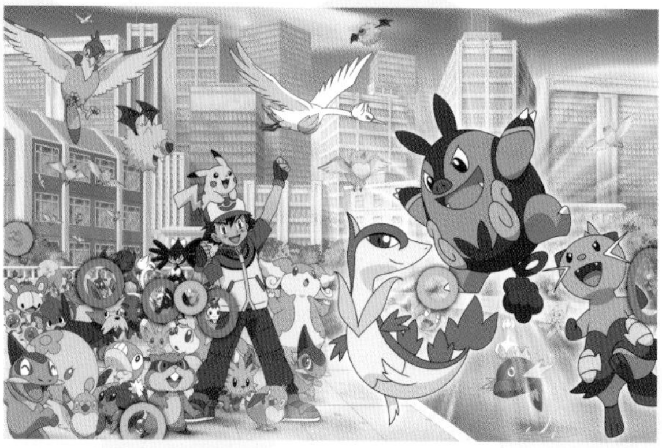

AT THE POKÉMON CENTER 9–10

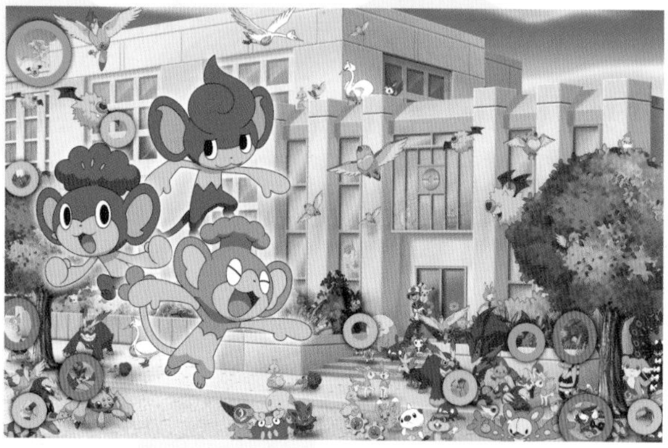

POKÉMON CENTER CHAOS 11–12

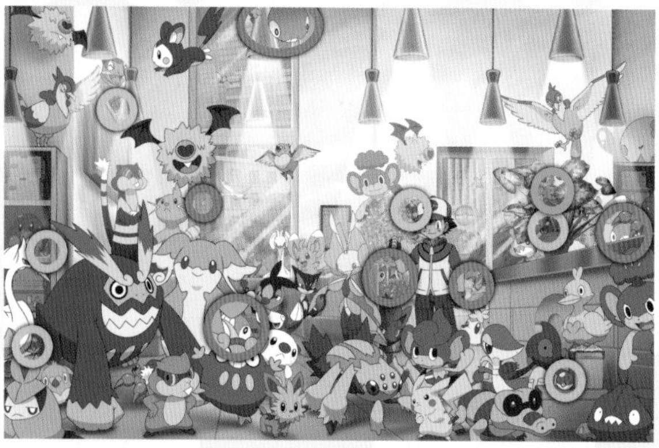

AFTER DARK 13–14

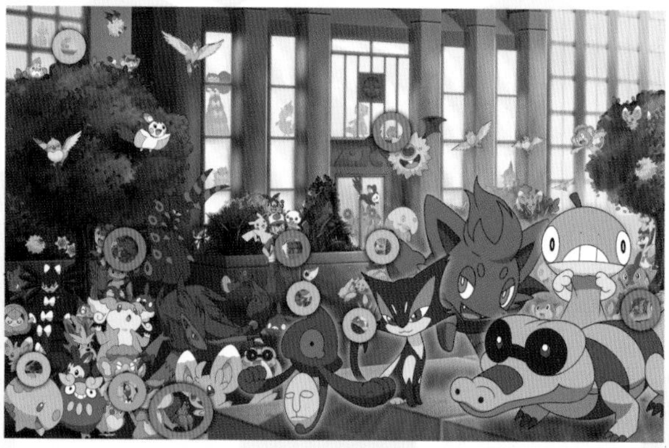

TIME FOR THE BATTLE CLUB 15–16

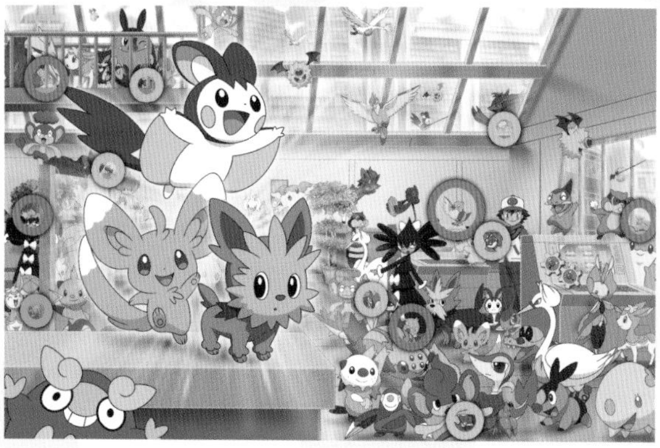

THE TRAINING ROOM 17–18

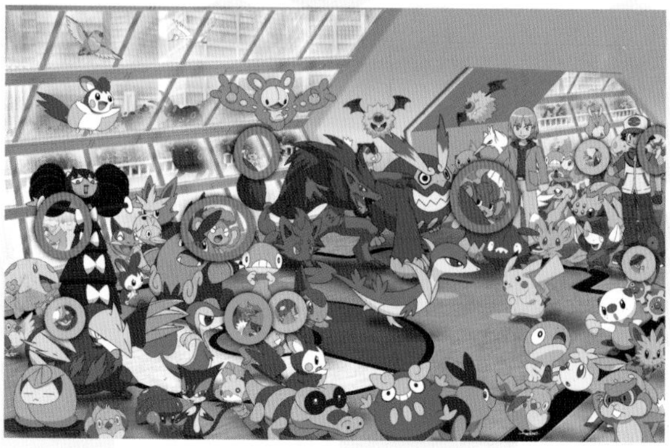

POKÉDEX POKÉMON POKÉ BALLS LEGENDARY POKÉMON

SOLUTIONS

A SUMMER MORNING 3–4

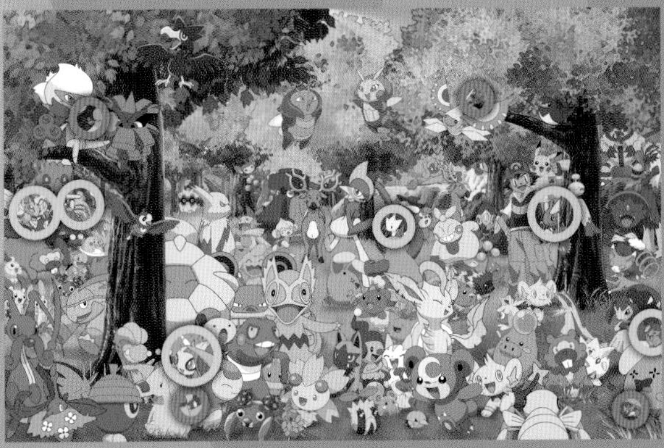

AN UNEXPECTED ENCOUNTER 5–6

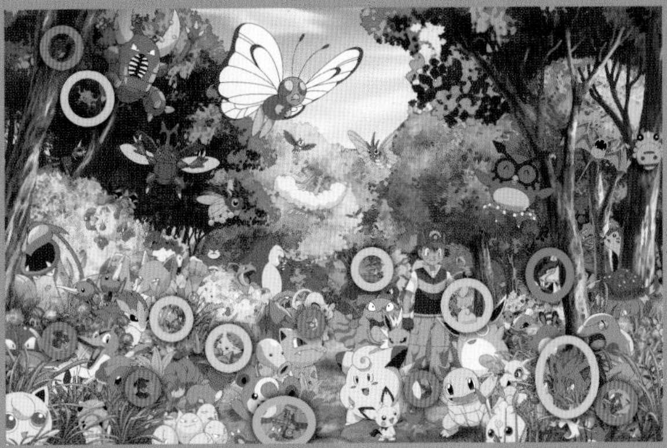

ON THE RIGHT TRACK 7–8

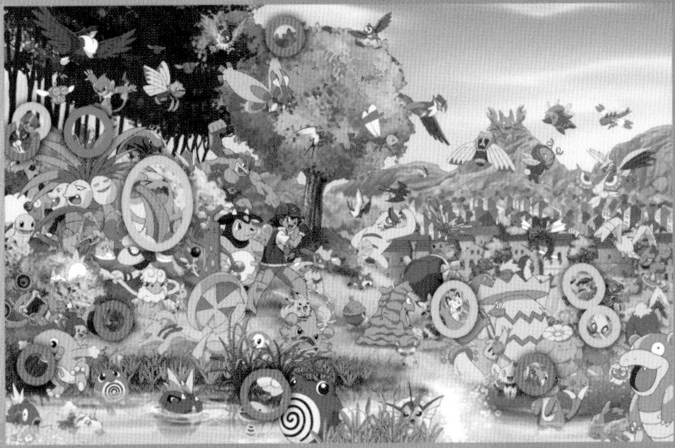

THE CREEK 9–10

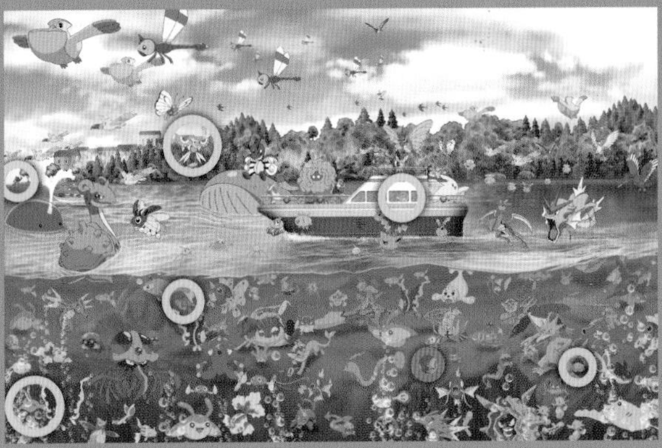

SEARCHING THE TOWN 11–12

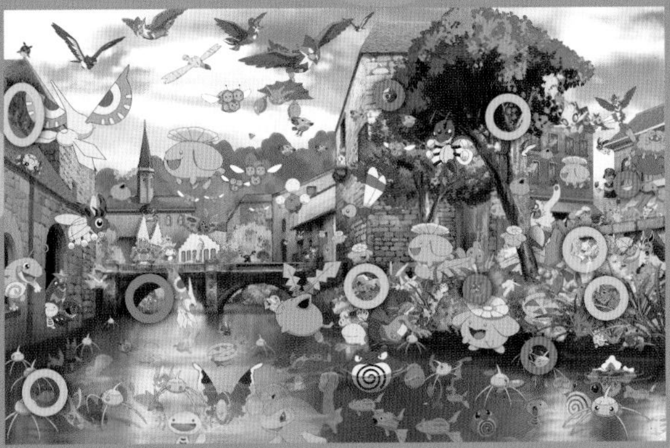

AT THE POKÉMON CENTER 13–14

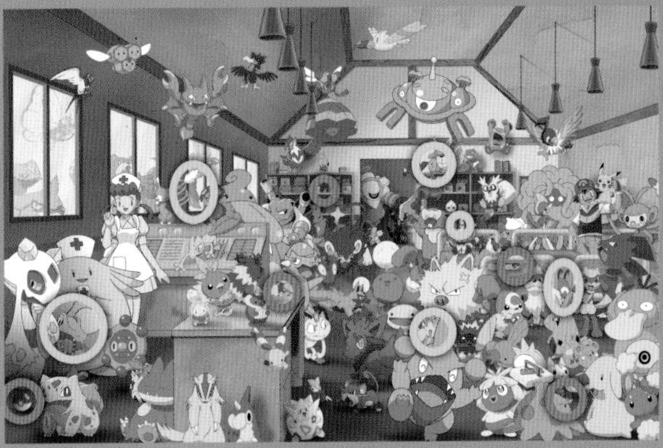

REUNION IN THE PARK 15–16

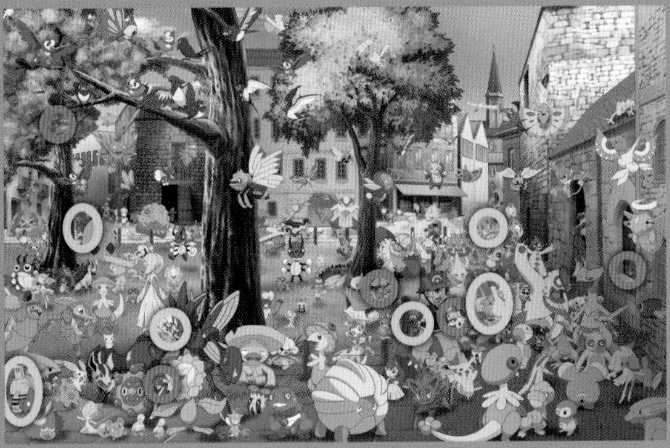

THE RETURN HOME 17–18

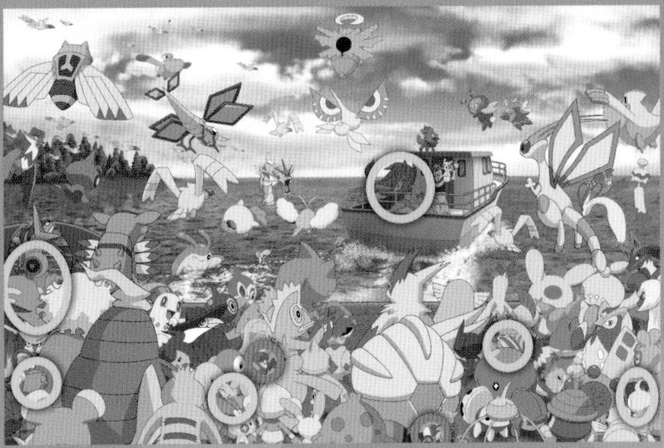

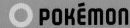

POKÉDEX   POKÉMON   POKÉ BALLS   LEGENDARY POKÉMON

ZOROARK

Like Zorua, Zoroark has the Illusion Ability, which lets it assume the appearance of any Pokémon.

TYPE: Dark
ABILITY: Illusion
HEIGHT: 5' 03" / 1,6m
WEIGHT: 178.8lbs. / 81,1kg

ZORUA

Zorua has the Illusion Ability, which lets it assume the appearance of other Pokémon and scare its enemies.

TYPE: Dark
ABILITY: Illusion
HEIGHT: 2' 04" / 0,7m
WEIGHT: 27.6lbs. / 12,5kg

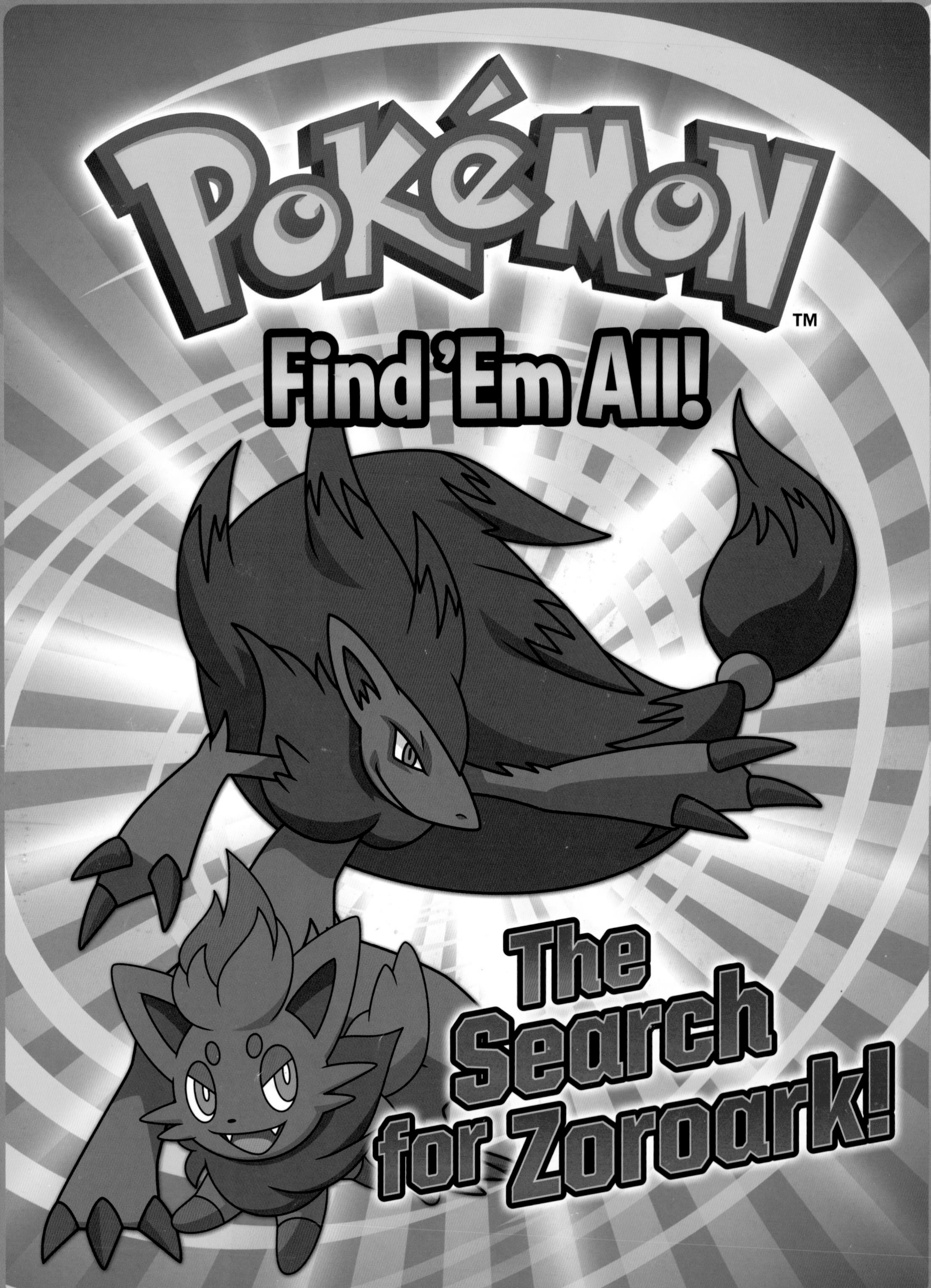

POKéMON™
Find 'Em All!
The Search for Zoroark!

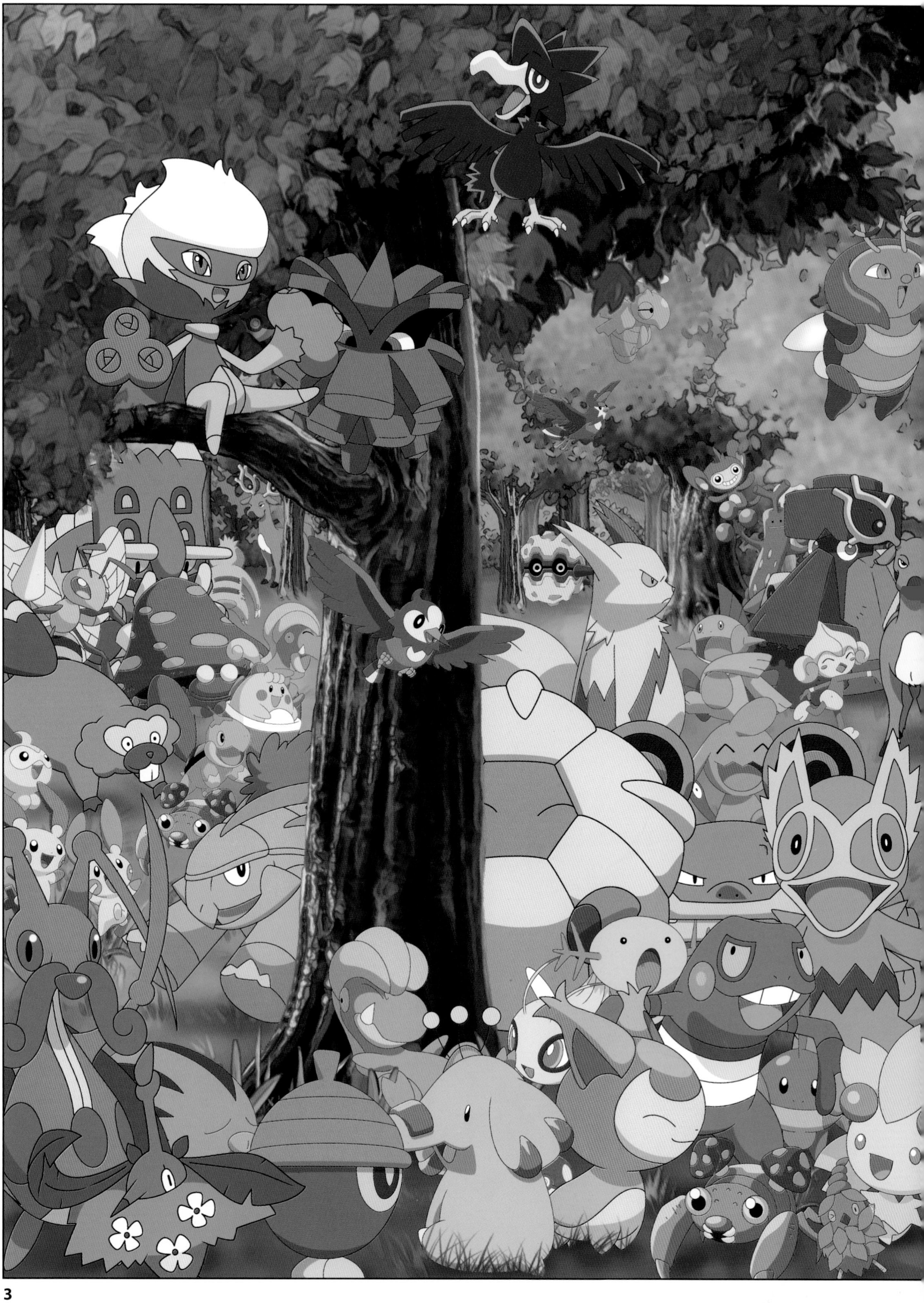

A SUMMER MORNING

One morning, many Pokémon showed up to play in the forest, enjoying the cool shade and having a good time. It can be hard to spot them; can you see where Slakoth, Lopunny, Togetic, Beedrill, and Bellossom are hiding? Celebi should be here, too—can you find Celebi?

x4

Find:

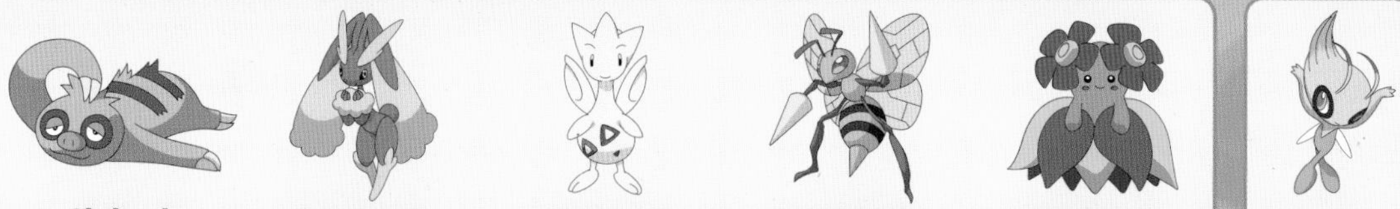

Slakoth | Lopunny | Togetic | Beedrill | Bellossom | Celebi

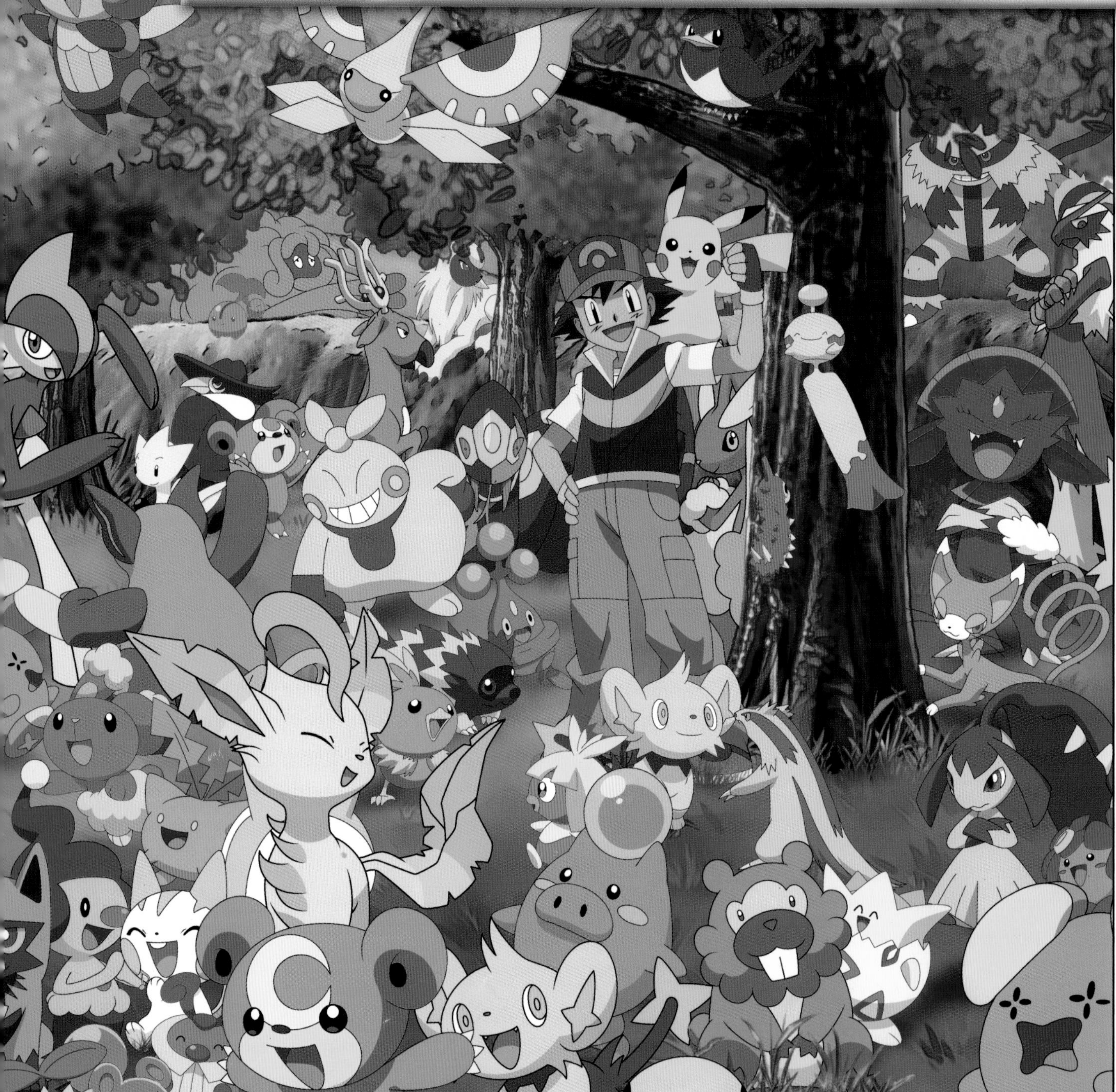

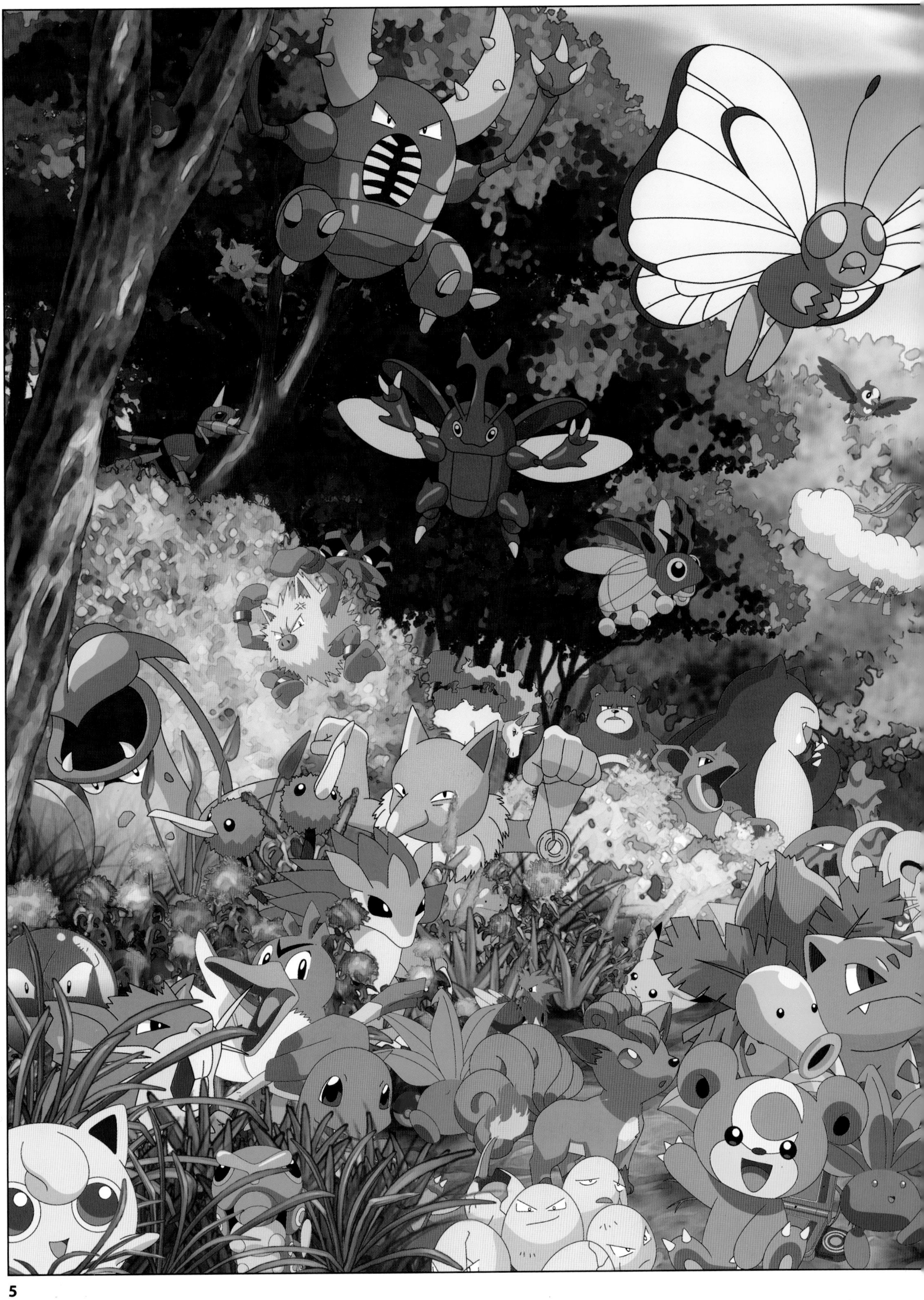

AN UNEXPECTED ENCOUNTER

On a shady path, Ash and his friends come face to face with a newcomer: Zorua, who seems to be lost. It's searching for Zoroark, the only one who knows how to get the two of them back to their home region. Ash decides to help Zorua, but first, you need to find these other Pokémon!

x6

Find:

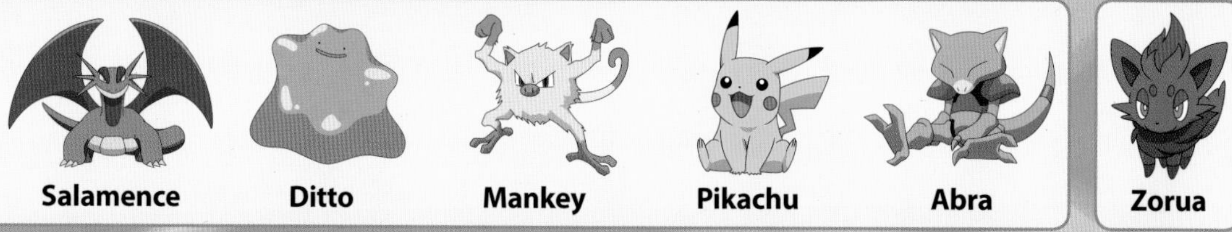
Salamence
Ditto
Mankey
Pikachu
Abra
Zorua

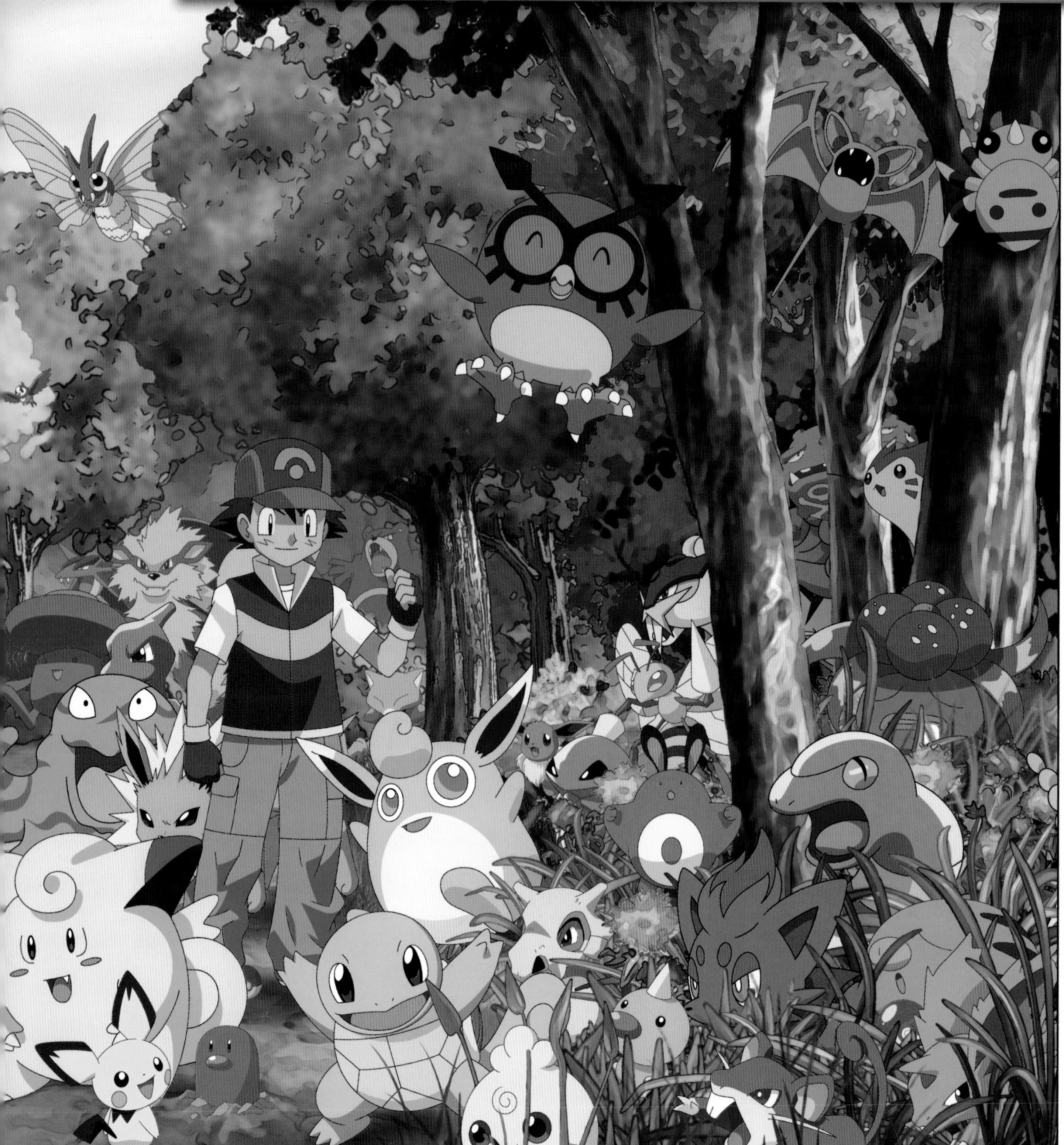

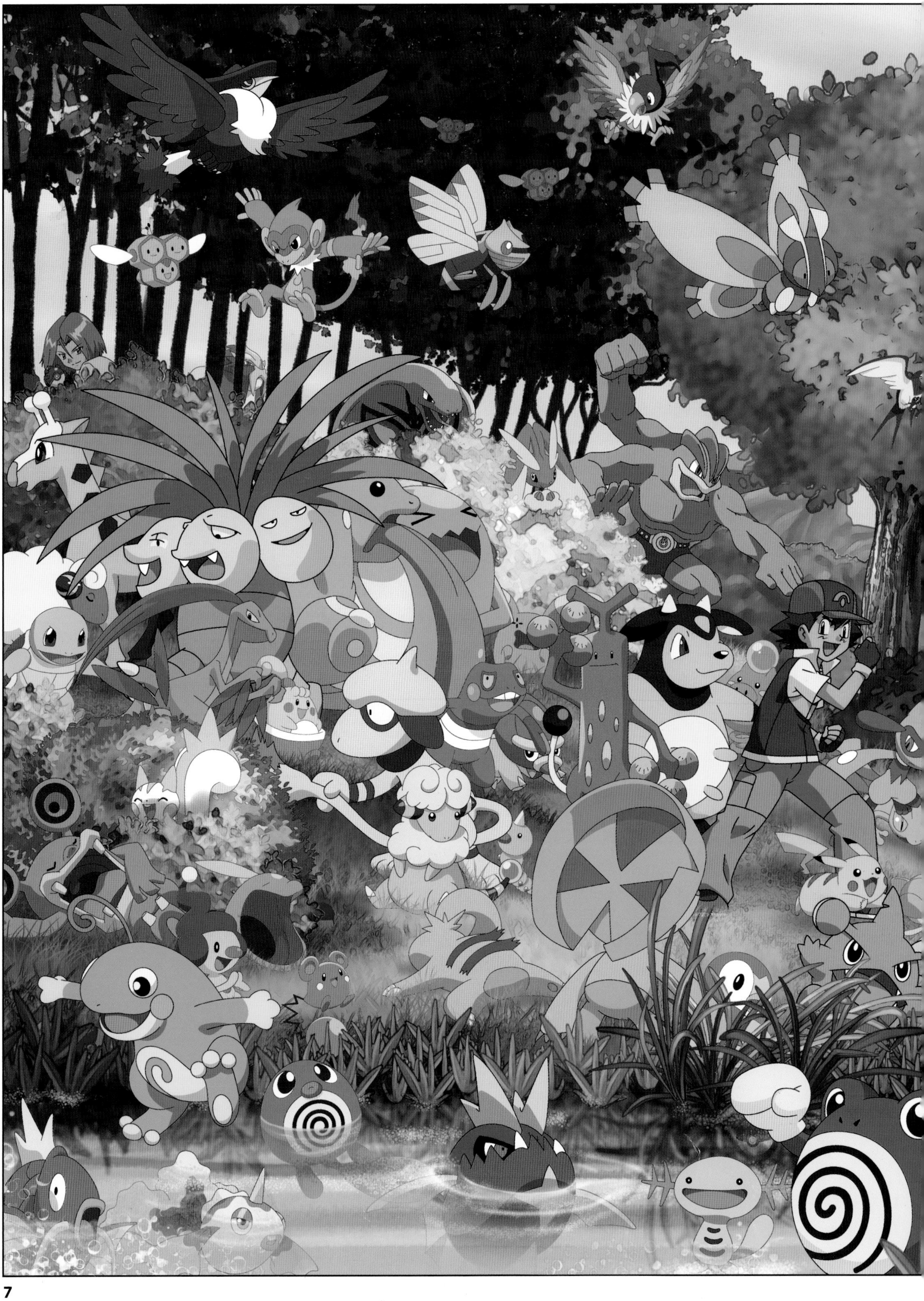

ON THE RIGHT TRACK

As they near the river, our heroes meet Celebi, who luckily will help them on their quest. Celebi will lead them to a town nearby where a mysterious Pokémon has recently been spotted. There's no time to lose!

Find:

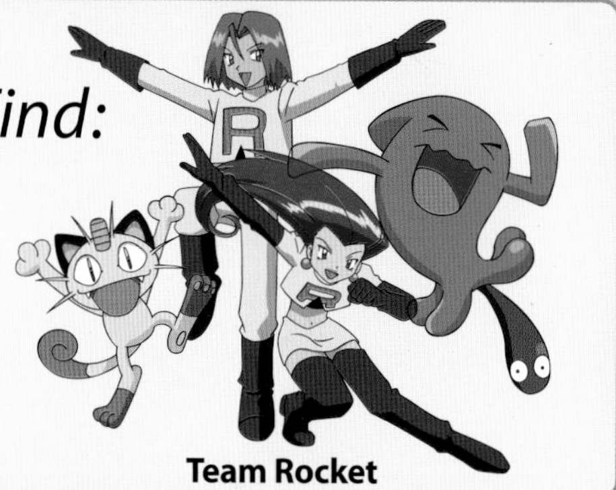

Team Rocket

x6

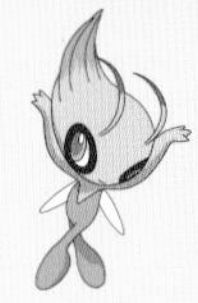

Celebi

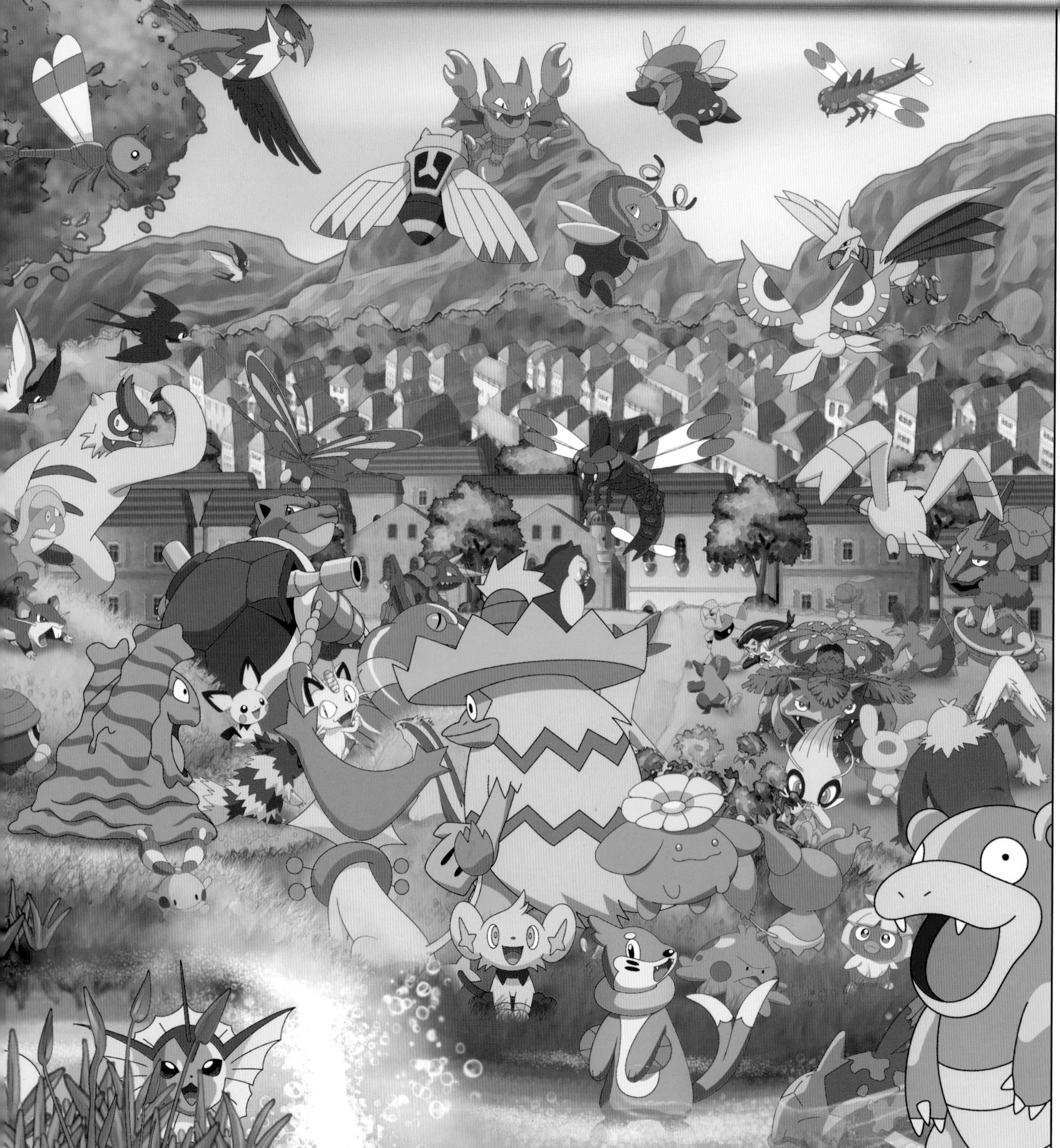

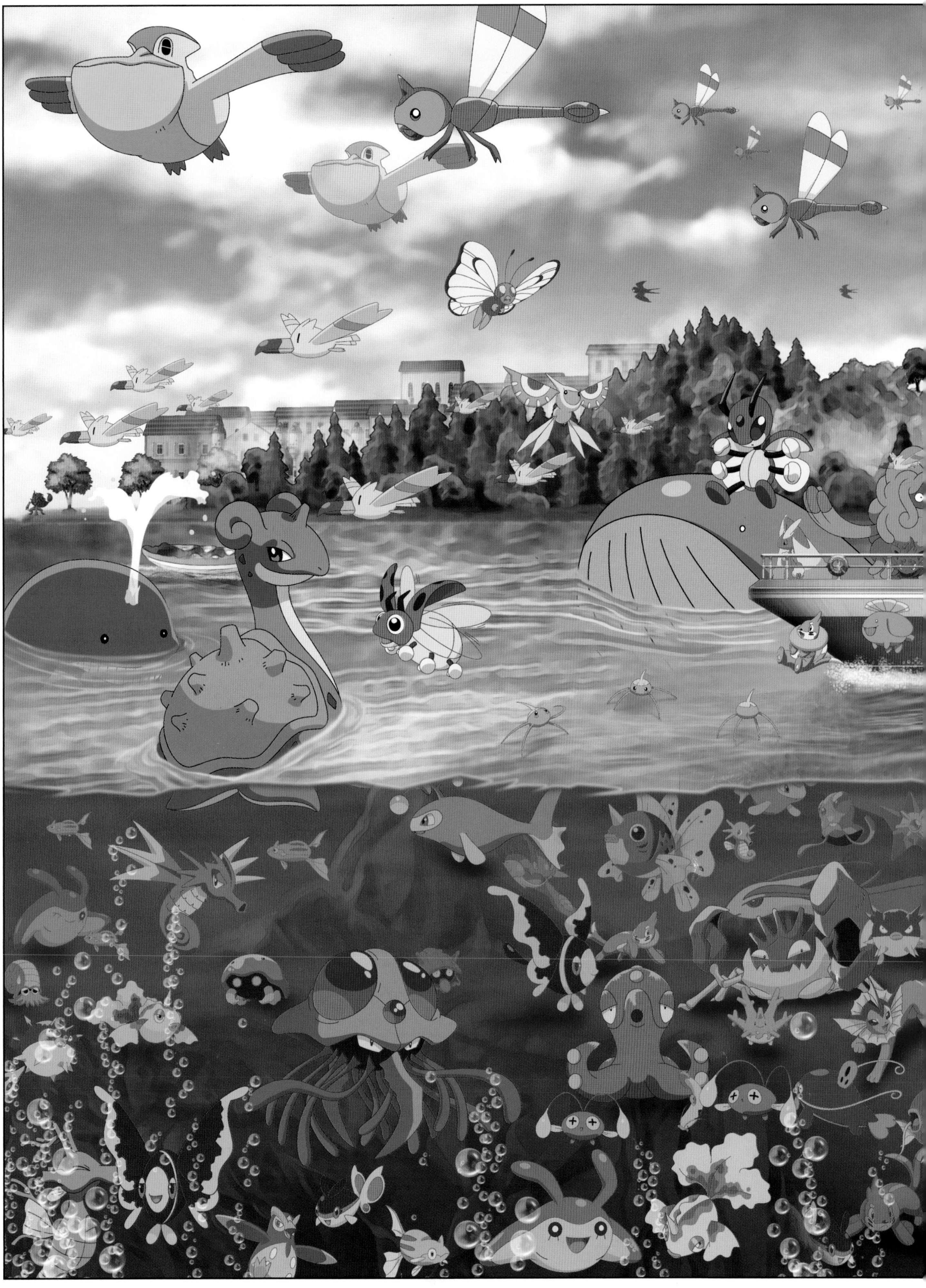

THE CREEK

The fastest way to reach the town is to go across the water. While on the boat, Ash asks all the Pokémon he meets for help and gathers more clues along the way. Have any of them seen Zoroark? Do you have any idea where Ash might find Zoroark?

x1

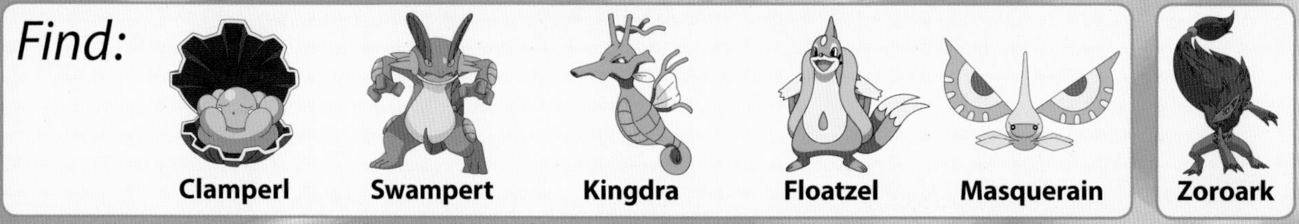
Find:
Clamperl
Swampert
Kingdra
Floatzel
Masquerain
Zoroark

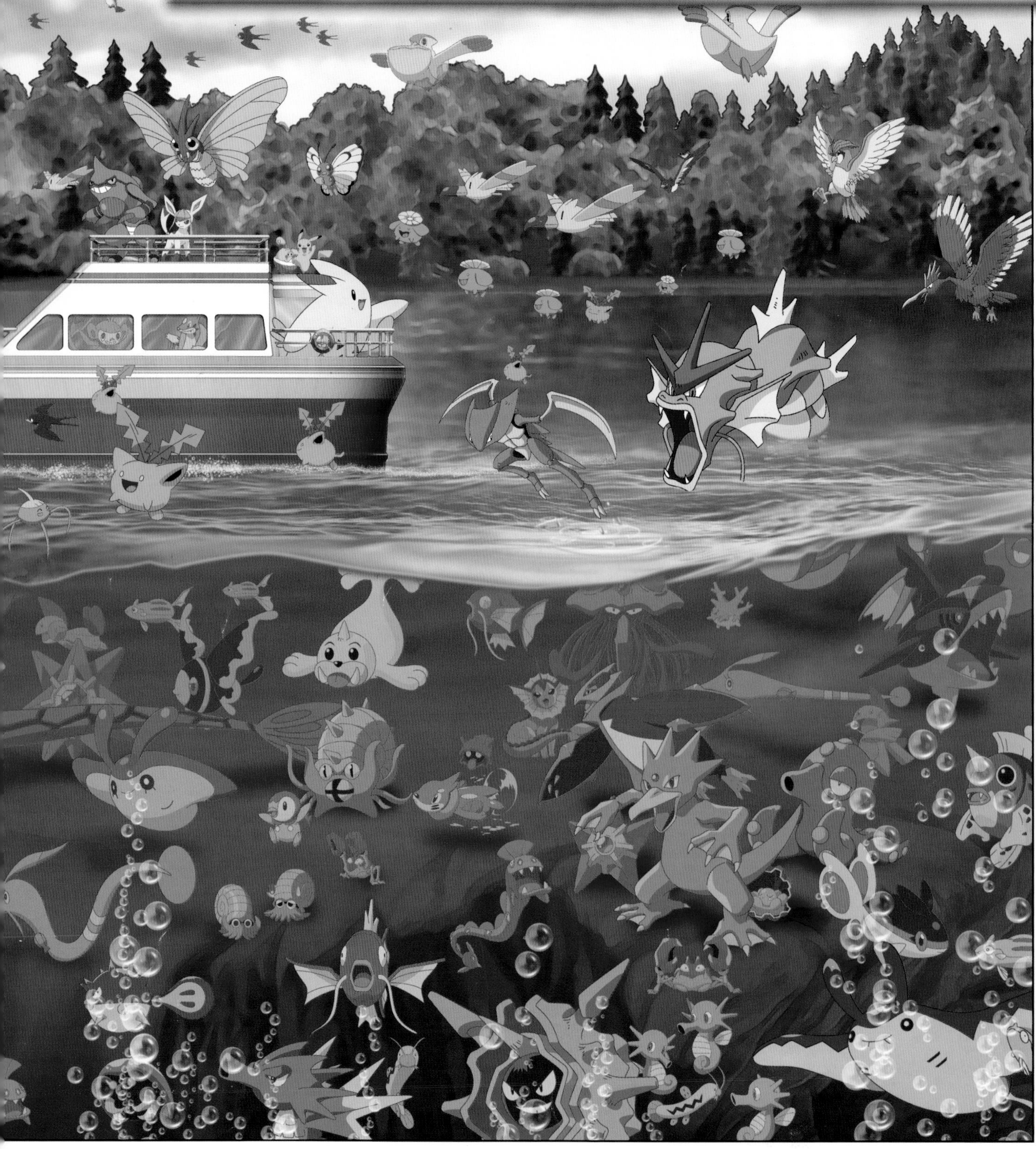

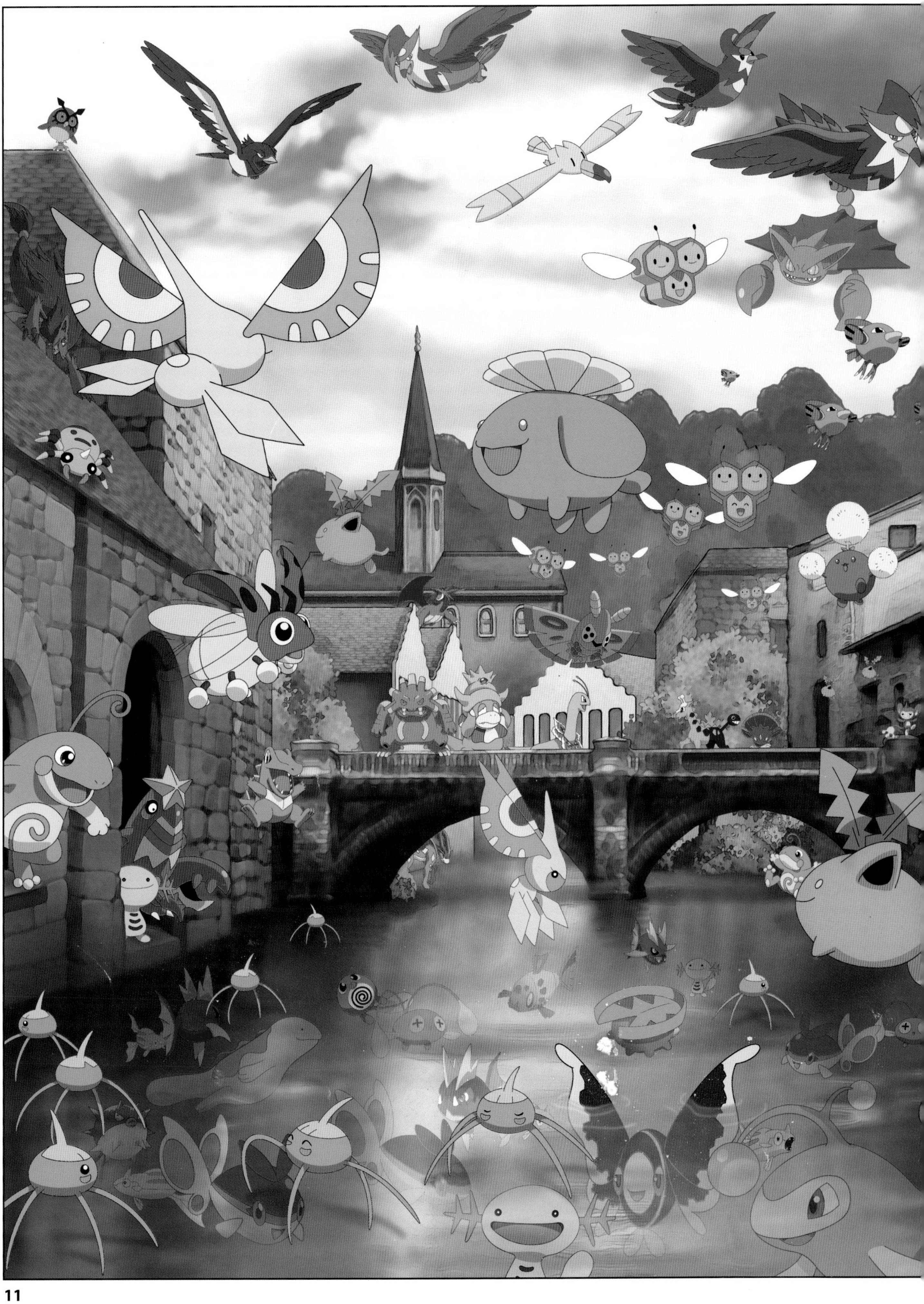

SEARCHING THE TOWN

Ash and his friends eventually reach the town, which is crisscrossed by bridges and canals. They wander the streets searching for Zoroark, but they have no luck. After all, it's not easy to find anything in the town's twists and turns when you're traveling with such a big crowd of Pokémon!

x4

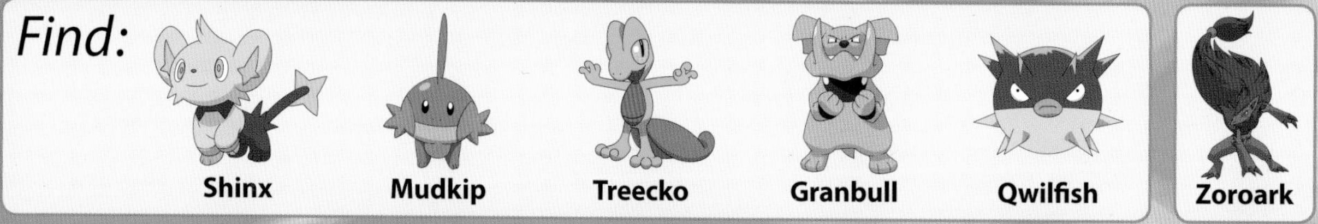

Find:
Shinx
Mudkip
Treecko
Granbull
Qwilfish
Zoroark

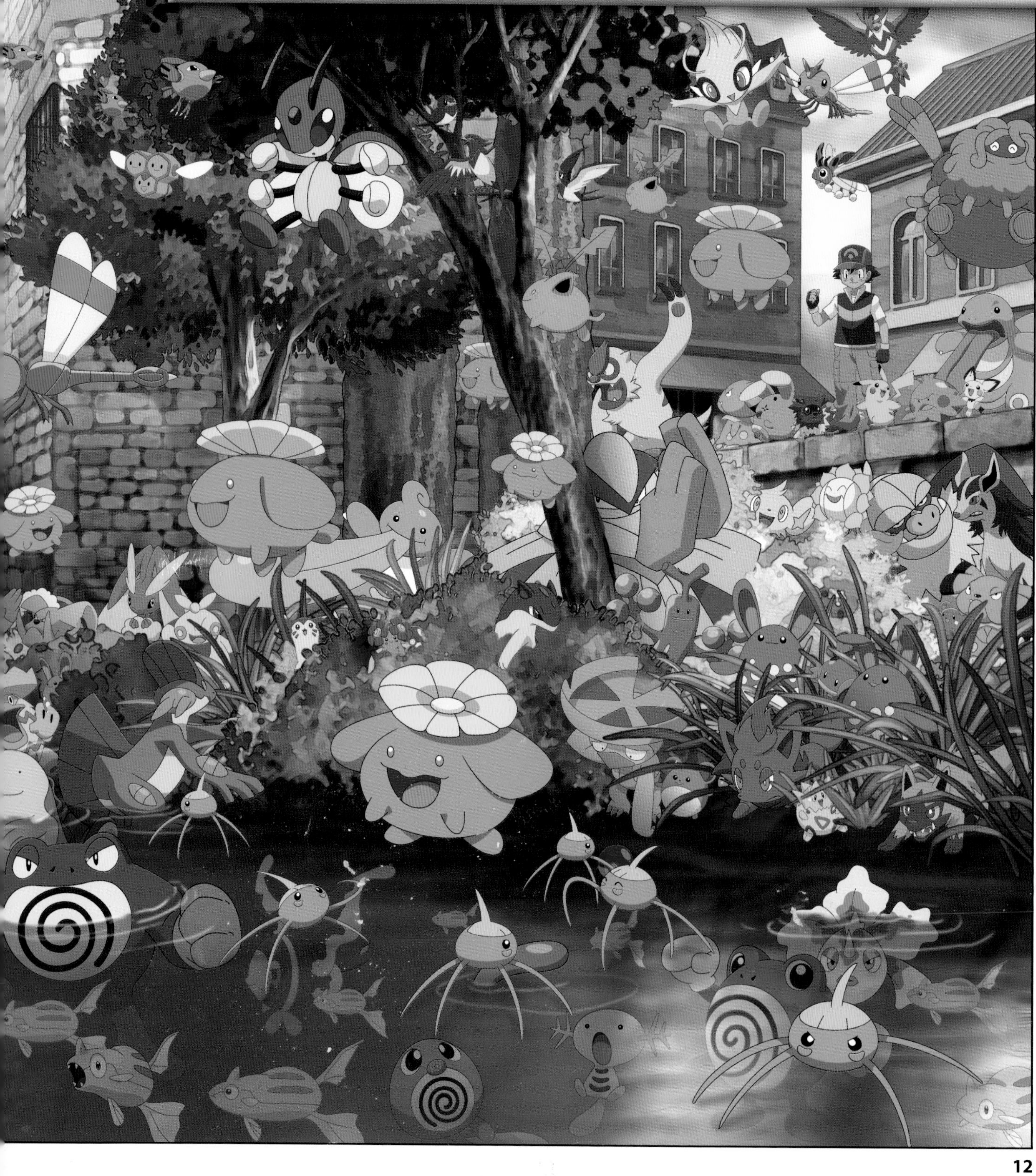

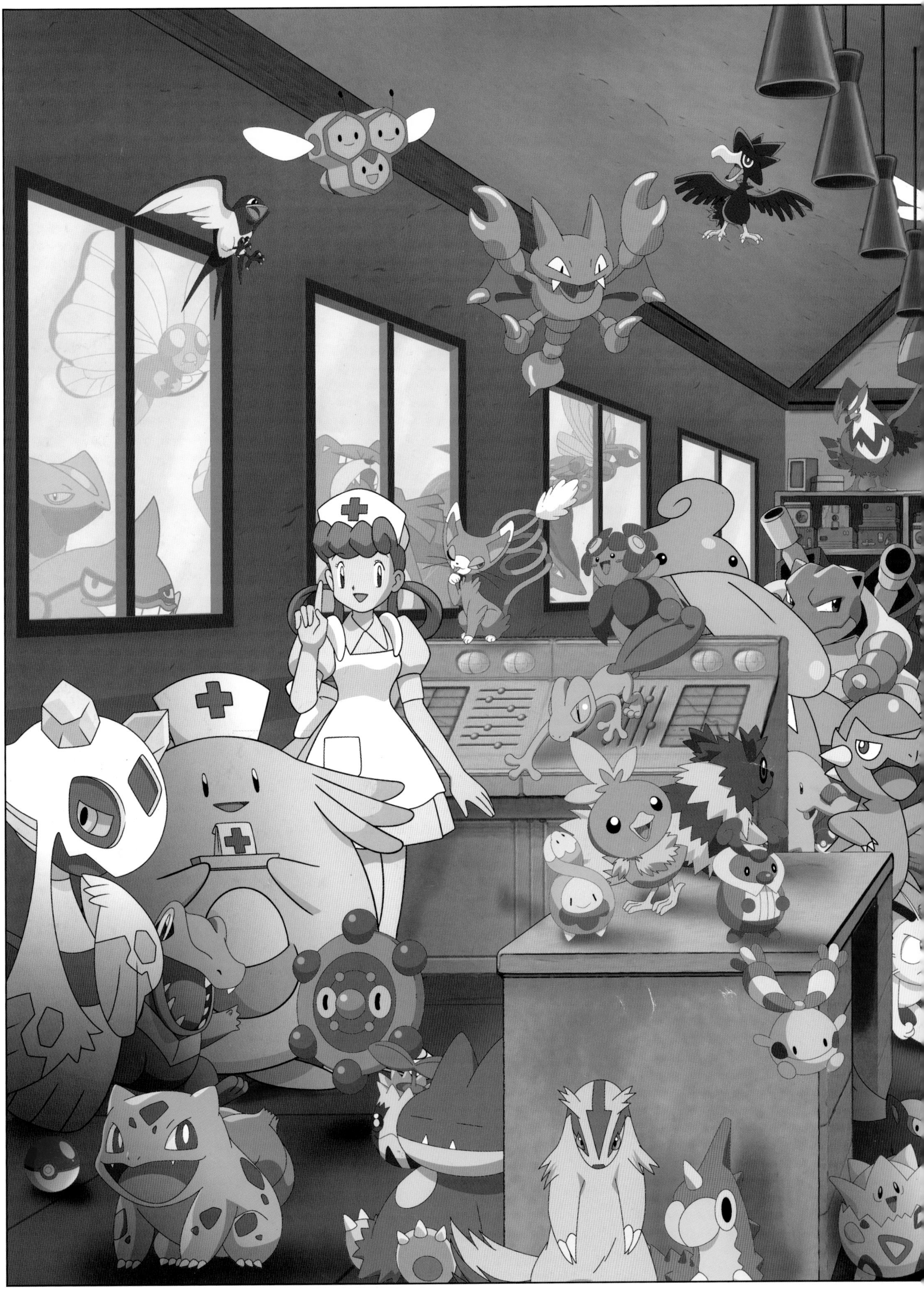

AT THE POKÉMON CENTER

Ash has an idea: the Pokémon Center is bound to have more information about the Pokémon he's looking for! Indeed, the team there tells him that a mysterious Pokémon has recently been seen in the town's park. Quick— let's go look for it there!

x5

Find:

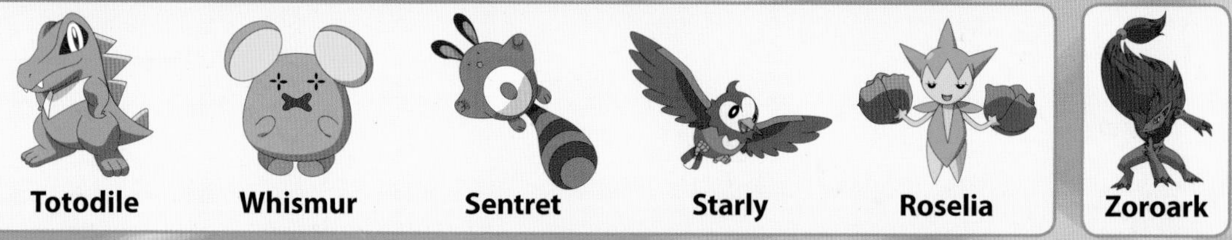
Totodile
Whismur
Sentret
Starly
Roselia
Zoroark

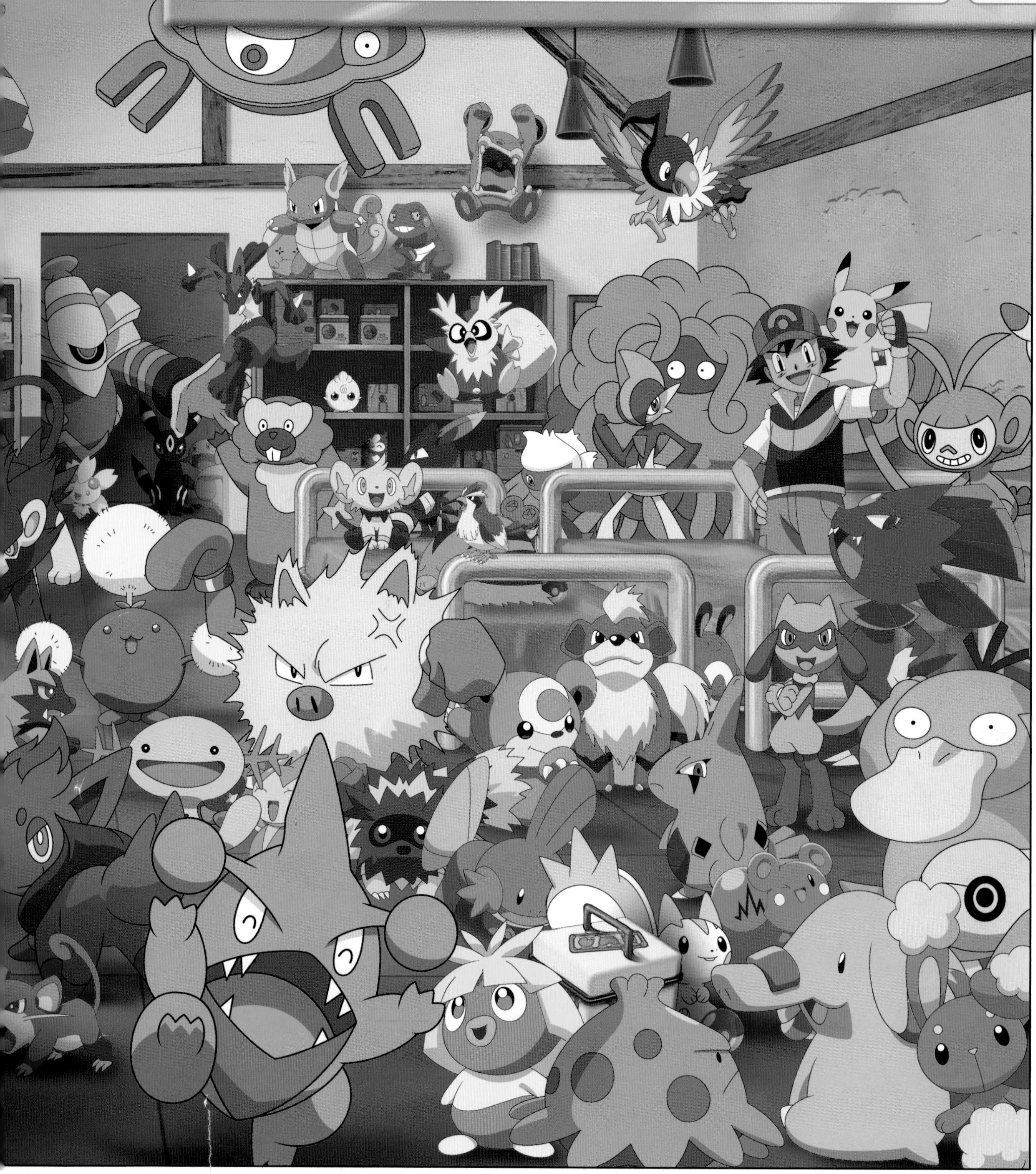

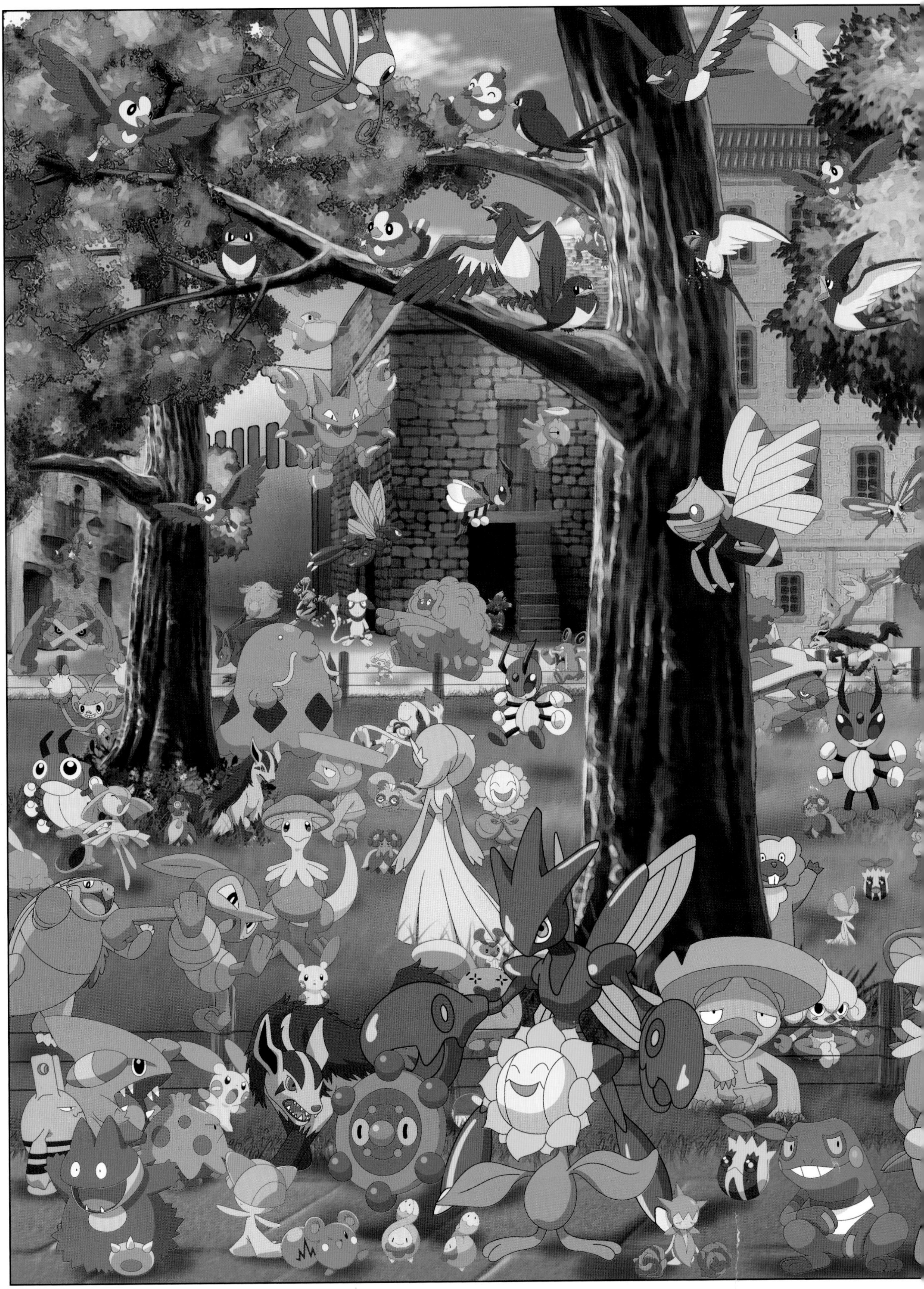

REUNION IN THE PARK

What a crowd in the park! After searching for some time, our friends finally find Zoroark. Can you spot Zoroark? Zorua is so happy—the two Pokémon will finally be able to go home! But in all the excitement, a few Pokémon got lost. Can you figure out where they're hiding?

x5

Find:

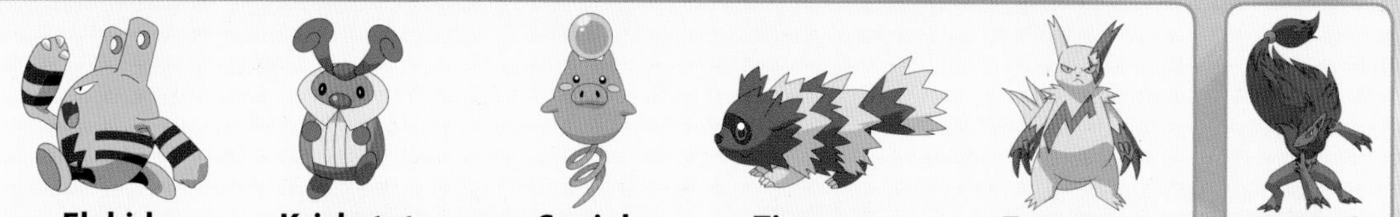

Elekid Kricketot Spoink Zigzagoon Zangoose Zoroark

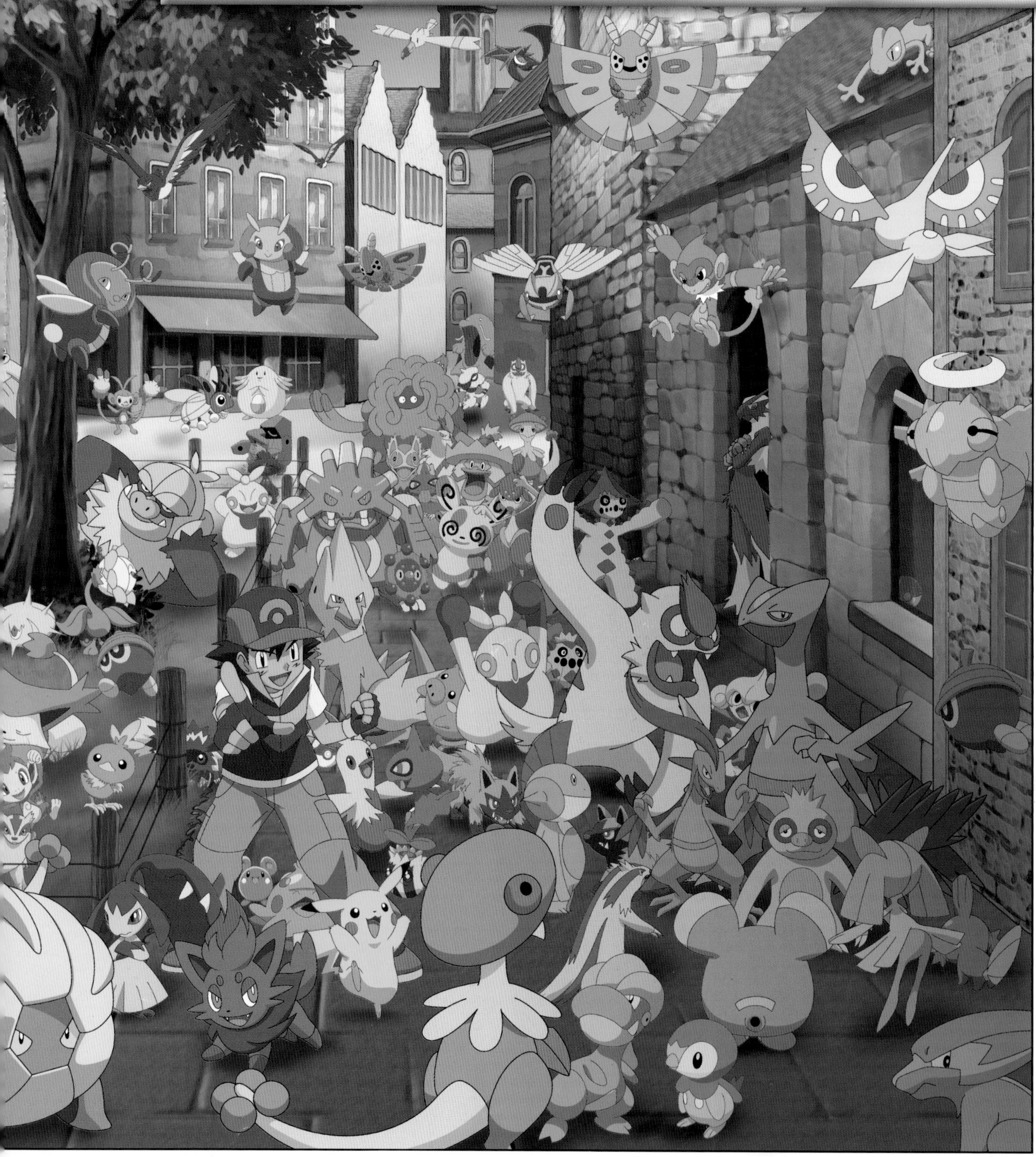

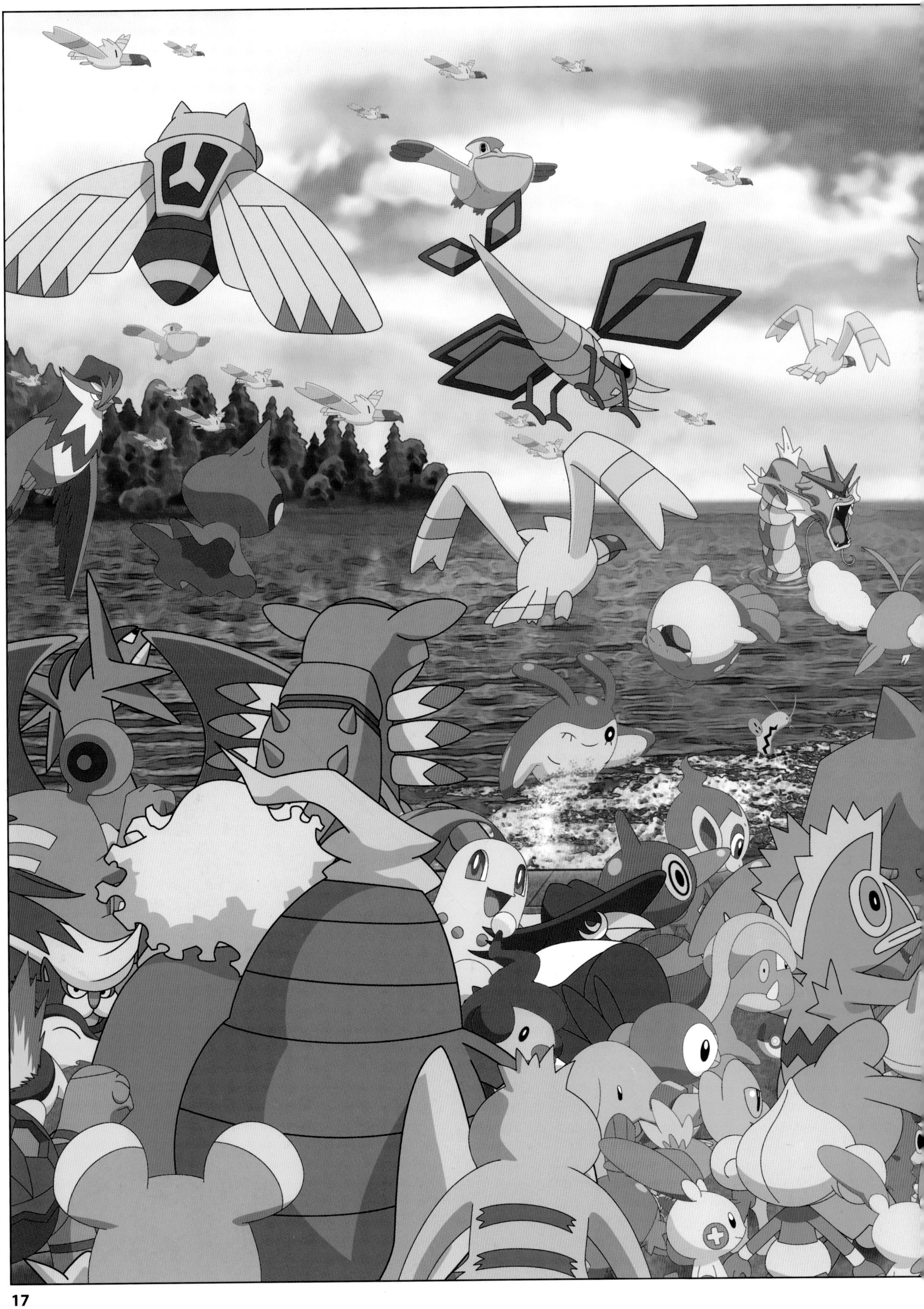

THE RETURN HOME

Zorua and Zoroark are very happy to finally be able to go back home. In the end, Ash decides to travel back with them by boat; he doesn't know anything about their home, and he's excited for the chance to check it out. As the other Pokémon wave goodbye, it's on to new adventures!

x2

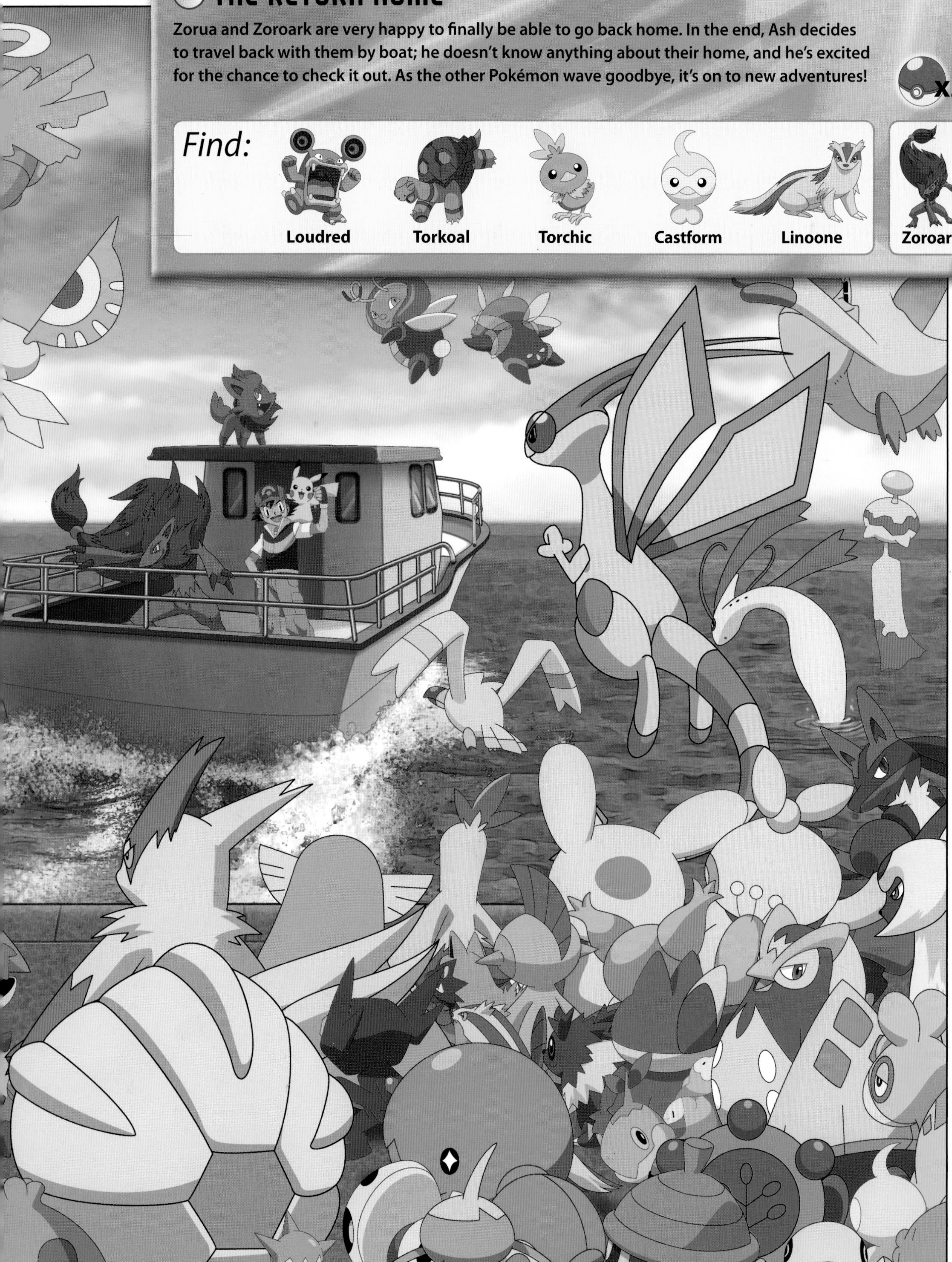

Find:
Loudred
Torkoal
Torchic
Castform
Linoone
Zoroark

NEW CHALLENGES

Have you completed every search and found all the Poké Balls?

Then you're ready for these two new challenges that only the best Pokémon Trainers can take on!

⊙ THE LEGENDARY CHALLENGE

Three Legendary Pokémon are hiding somewhere in these pages of adventure. Can you find them?

Suicune

Entei

Raikou

⊙ THE SUPREME CHALLENGE

During his adventure, Ash dropped his Pokédex, which allows him to collect data and learn all about Pokémon. Help him figure out where he lost it!

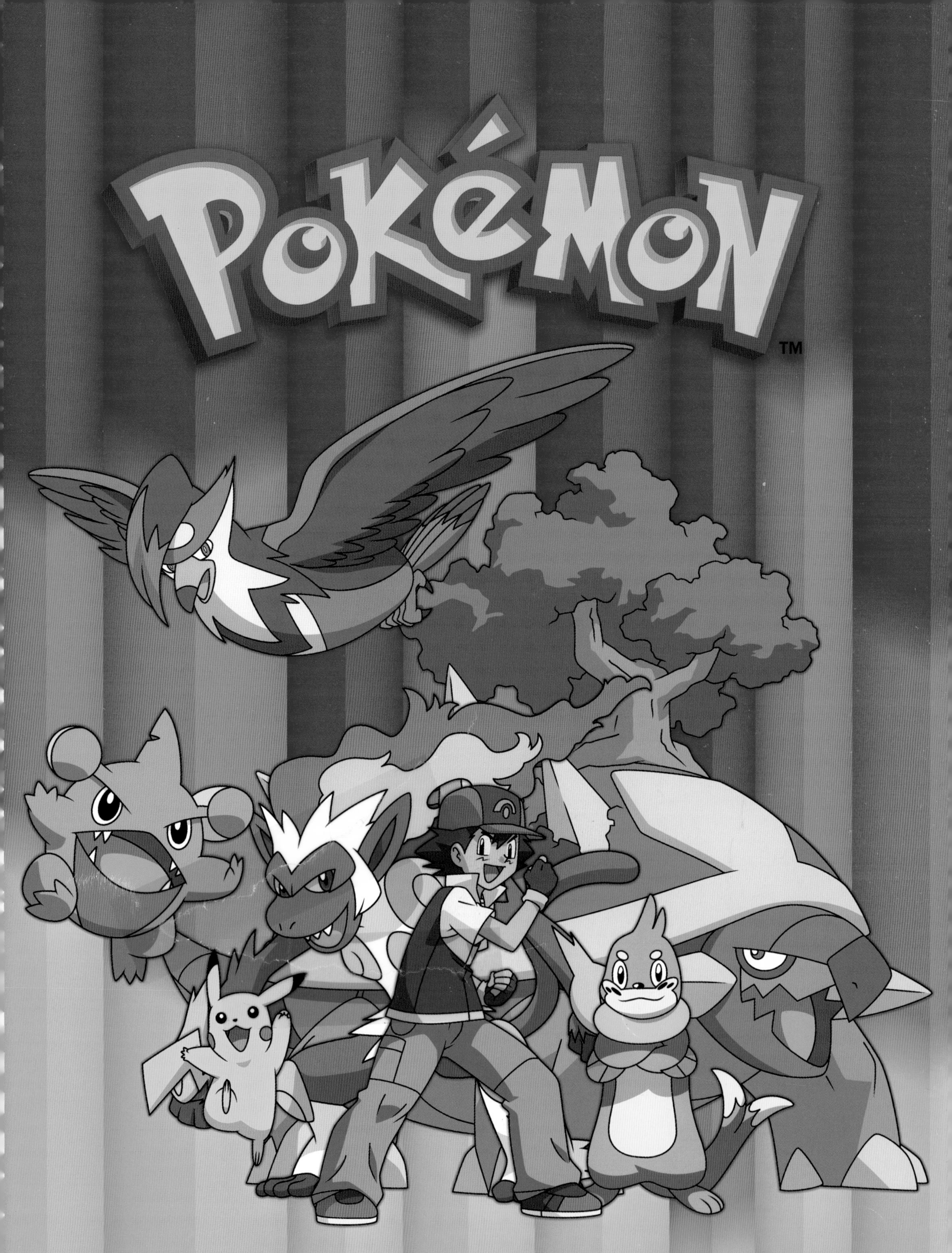
POKÉMON™